D0855919

DYING FOR YOU

Geraldine Evans titles available from Severn House Large Print

Absolute Poison
Up in Flames

DYING FOR YOU

Geraldine Evans

Severn House Large Print
London & New York

This first large print edition published in Great Britain 2006 by
SEVERN HOUSE LARGE PRINT BOOKS LTD of
9-15 High Street, Sutton, Surrey, SM1 1DF.
First world regular print edition published 2004 by
Severn House Publishers, London and New York.
This first large print edition published in the USA 2006 by
SEVERN HOUSE PUBLISHERS INC., of
595 Madison Avenue, New York, NY 10022.

British Library Cataloguing in Publication Data

Evans, Geraldine
Dying for you. - Large print ed. – (Rafferty and Llewellyn crime series)
1. Rafferty, Joseph (Fictitious character) - Fiction
2. Llewellyn, Sergeant (Fictitious character) - Fiction
3. Police - Great Britain - Fiction
4. Detective and mystery stories
5. Large type books
I. Title
823.9'14 [F]

ISBN-10: 0-7278-7501-9

Printed and bound in Great Britain by
MPG Books Ltd, Bodmin, Cornwall.

One

Only a few days earlier...

Rafferty hovered on the pavement opposite Made In Heaven's Hope Street office, garnering courage while he essayed fascination with the pharmacy's window display. Finally, alert for familiar faces, he crossed the road and walked under the agency's sign of cherubs playing hide and seek amongst billowing white clouds and through the rose-tinted glass of the dating agency's door.

Inside was a large and airy outer office, its walls hung with dreamy, soft-focus wedding photographs. Half-a-dozen easy chairs in soft pastel shades were grouped around low coffee tables bestrewn with magazines that followed the walls' romantic theme.

All the *faux*-romantic ambience made Rafferty want to turn tail and run. Maybe he would have done, but the pink-suited buxom blonde behind the reception desk raised her head from her magazine for long enough to smile at him with eyes that didn't focus properly on his face and asked if she could help him.

'I've got a 2 p.m. appointment with Ms Durward.' Rafferty took a deep breath. 'Name of Blythe. Nigel Blythe.'

The receptionist, her nose inches from the appointment diary, found his name and ticked it off. 'Ms Durward will be free shortly. Please take a seat.'

Rafferty selected an easy chair with its back to the window, picked up one of the magazines and began to flick through the pages. Much like the 'wedded bliss' pictures on the walls the magazine featured impossibly beautiful brides, gazing adoringly at their equally handsome grooms. He closed the magazine with a snap loud enough for the receptionist to raise her head from her own magazine and gaze in his general direction.

Just then, a young man appeared from a short corridor off reception. He was good-looking with a cock-of-the-walk stride. The receptionist welcomed him fulsomely, calling him 'Darius'. He called her 'Isobel' and continued a conversation about his recent travels that must have started when he had first arrived. Isobel's sole contribution to the conversation was a liberal application of '*absolutely*s' and '*fab*s' and '*groovy*s' every time there was a tiny pause. But as Darius seemed principally interested in talking about himself there were few enough of these. Thankfully, Darius must have had other urgent monologue engagements that day because he left shortly after.

Once he had gone, Isobel turned her attentions to Rafferty. Artlessly, she confided, 'Darius is the son of one of Mummy's friends. He lives in the most wonderful style. Don't know how he affords it as according to his file he doesn't work and has no private means at all. Well, apart from the little importing firm he told me about.' She giggled. 'Said he'd let me have some coke at cost. Wasn't that darling of him?'

'Absolutely,' said Rafferty.

The intercom on Isobel's desk beeped, Isobel confirmed Nigel Blythe had arrived and was asked to send him through.

Rafferty walked along the short corridor, found the office, knocked and was bidden to enter. Caroline Durward stood up and came round her desk to introduce herself. Rafferty placed her around the mid-thirties. Tall, three or four inches under Rafferty's six foot, she was a little overweight, but it was extra poundage she carried with dignity. On the plain side, with a prominent nose, her make-up, though heavy, had been expertly applied to make the most of her assets of flawless skin and clear grey eyes. In contrast to the romantic decor, she wore a business-like skirt suit in a brisk navy. She invited him to sit in front of her desk – a delicate-looking construction with ormolu gilding, the obligatory computer perched incongruously on top.

After he had handed over the form that had been posted to him for completion at home she glanced quickly through it and told him with a smile, 'That seems to be in order.'

Rafferty shifted uncomfortably on his chair as Caroline Durward began to enter 'his' details on the computer, for although her manner was friendly, she put him in mind of Miss Robson, the deputy head from his junior school days. She had shared Ms Durward's well-modulated diction. It hadn't stopped her from putting the fear of God into the young Rafferty and his classmates – literally, as she was the Religious Instruction teacher. She had insisted they learn great tracts of the Bible by heart and would send the blackboard rubber flying towards the head of the child who failed. So while half of Rafferty was trying to remember he was meant to be a cool middle-class dude, the other half prepared to duck.

A tiny frown marred the previous smooth perfection of Caroline's forehead. Rafferty guessed she had come to the section of his form that was liberally daubed with correction fluid. And as she glanced at Nigel's passport photograph, Rafferty presented her with his best 'Nigel' profile and gazed around him at the walls of the office which were decorated with yet more wedding photographs. He suspected they were mock-ups. Sensibly, he had made enquiries and discovered the agency had only been set up six months previously; scarcely time enough for so much wedded bliss to have occurred, he thought. There was even one such photo on Caroline Durward's desk, but as this one lost the dreamy soft-focus and featured a plain bride who was undoubtedly the younger version of Caroline Durward, with a groom whose eyes were so screwed up against the sun that his features were distorted, he guessed this marriage was real enough.

By now, Caroline Durward had bravely fought her way to the end of his form and had 'his' details entered on her computer. She looked brightly at him and said, 'Now, Mr Blythe – or may I call you Nigel?' At Rafferty's nod, she said, 'Do call me Caroline. We like to keep things friendly here.' She went on to enlarge upon the information he had received through the post. 'As our literature states, we're a small, select agency. We serve the professional classes.'

Rafferty kept his face straight as Caroline's rather heavy features darted an unconscious little moue towards his unprofessionally completed form, before she continued, even more brightly. 'Apart from the guarantee of a minimum of two introductions, you'll be able to attend our regular parties and other functions – trips to the theatre, weekends away in Paris, Amsterdam and so on, so you will have the opportunity to meet as many of our members as care to attend. We also have many action-packed trips and weekends for our more physically inclined clientele. I see from your form, Nigel, you're not much into physical pursuits.'

This last helped a tiny line force its way through the make-up. Tiny flakes of powder sat on top of it as if for emphasis. Rafferty began to feel he was becoming something of a disappointment to Caroline Durward. Quickly, he assured her, 'I was sporty when I was younger. But nowadays I get little time.'

'Time – always a problem for our members. Most of them lead such hectic lives. That's where we come in, of course. Like that old advert that claimed its product took the waiting out of wanting we try to do the same. And as an independent agency rather than part of a large chain, we're able to offer that important personal touch. We keep our gatherings small, usually no more than fifty, occasionally as many as a hundred, but never more than that. We mostly hold our regular "Getting-to-Know-You" parties at my own home, so much more intimate than the usual hotel function rooms.'

Rafferty had a picture in his mind of one hundred people crammed way-too-intimately into a standard three-bed semi. But Caroline soon reassured him.

'Of course, my home, New Hall, is large enough to offer intimacy to such numbers without a crush. I think you'll find it attractive. Most people seem to. But its main advantage is that it makes for much more discretion than the more usual busy hotel locations, though we also make use of facilities at local four-star hotels, like The Elmhurst. We find their annexe convenient as it's set in its own grounds apart from the main hotel so gives the privacy our members require.'

Rafferty relaxed so much under Caroline's practised sales patter that he forgot his reservations and told her he was happy to sign up.

A few minutes later, she stood up, shook his hand and as she ushered him to the door, told him, 'Isobel, our receptionist, will take your fee and give you the personal invitations for our current social functions, a list of sensible guidelines, as well as a detailed map of Elmhurst and surrounds. We have two of our "Getting-to-Know-You" parties coming up imminently. As you'll have learned from our literature, we hold a number of these each month to introduce new clients to the other members. Promise you won't be shy and will attend at least one of these parties?'

Rafferty promised, which seemed to earn him an approving smile.

'Good. Good. Some of our clients tend to need the "mother hen" approach,' she confided. 'That's more the province of Simon Farnell, another of the agency partners. Simon does "mother hen" very well.'

Briefly, her eyes flickered with something that was far from a match for the lovey-dovey wedding pictures. Rafferty guessed that, like most businesses, the partners were at loggerheads about something. However, unlike her receptionist, Caroline Durward didn't treat him to gossipy confidences as to what it was about Simon Farnell's 'mother hen' approach to which she took exception.

They said their goodbyes and as Rafferty reached the second door in the short corridor it opened and a slim, fair-haired young man emerged. He gave Rafferty a wide smile.

'A new member, I see. Let me introduce myself. I'm Simon Farnell, one of the partners. And you are?'

'Nigel Blythe.' So this was the 'mother hen', Rafferty thought. Farnell had the indefinable camp air and exquisite tailoring that proclaimed 'homosexual'.

'Good to meet you, Nigel.' Farnell propped himself against the wall and stuffed his hands nonchalantly in his pockets as though preparing for a neighbourly gossip. He must have noticed Rafferty's frowning glance at the wedding pictures that also lined the walls of the corridor, for he quickly reassured, in a voice that must surely be heard through the panels of Caroline's office door, 'Don't be put off by all the fake wedding pictures. I told Caroline they were a mistake, but she insisted they were necessary to create the right ambience. They might have been convincing, too, as I told her, if we'd been going for several years. But as it is—' He broke off and sighed in a long-suffering manner that implied some people couldn't be told anything. He again shook Rafferty's hand with both of his and told him, 'But I mustn't keep you. I expect you're busy, busy, busy like so many of our other clients.'

As Rafferty removed his hand from Simon Farnell's over-effusive handshake and re-entered reception, he wrinkled his nose. He hadn't previously noticed how cloying was the perfume Isobel favoured. There should be a law, he often thought, to stop people imposing their penchant for powerful pongs on the nostrils of others.

At least Isobel didn't seem inclined to chat and force him to linger, for which he was grateful. She was engrossed in the magazine that, like the rest piled in the open drawer of her desk, featured exotic honeymoon destinations and wildly expensive country house receptions. She seemed to find them absorbing, but she forced her head up for long enough – with much fumbling and peering at the numbers – to put Nigel's credit card through her machine. She handed him the personal party invitations, the guidelines and the map of Elmhurst with New Hall, Caroline Durward's home, The Elmhurst and a couple of other prestigious venues boldly marked. After giving him a dreamy, unfocused, far-away goodbye, she retreated to her magazine, obviously already back on some sun-drenched beach with the perfect lover even before Rafferty had got the door open.

Two

Only a couple of days later Rafferty sat in The Huntsman, one of several riverside pubs in Elmhurst. It wasn't one of his usual haunts, being a bit upmarket, modern and, with its vast selection of alcopops, clearly designed to appeal to the younger generation. But, keen to get into his 'Nigel' persona, he had thought it the sort of place that would appeal to Nigel, though when he'd checked with his cousin that this wasn't one of his preferred drinking holes, Nigel had laughed the idea to scorn down Rafferty's borrowed mobile.

Unwilling to arrive at the Made In Heaven party smelling of drink with the appearance of needing Dutch courage, he'd bought orange juice instead of his customary Jameson's or pint of Adnams. Trouble was, Dutch courage was exactly what he needed. But then again, as he stared at the healthy juice with distaste, he hadn't totally made up his mind that he was *going*.

Don't start that again, he told himself. Besides, he'd ordered a taxi, from an unfamiliar cab firm; he'd even remembered to order it in his 'Nigel' persona.

To put a stop to any further prevarication, as he saw a man enter and the barman nod in his direction, he picked up the glass, drank the contents in one swallow and after hailing the cabbie, followed him out of the pub with a determined stride. The early April evening was muggy, threatening a storm. He smiled as he wondered what the honeymooning Sergeant Llewellyn would say if he had seen his DI drinking orange juice. The smile faded as he wondered what his ma would *do* if she ever found out about his signing up with the agency. But he was determined she would never find out; not Ma, nor anyone else. It was his secret and he intended it to stay that way. Well, his and Jerry's.

Caroline Durward's home, New Hall, the venue for the evening's party, was the other side of the village of St Botolphe to the south-east of Elmhurst. Rafferty had done a recce which had revealed the presence of a security camera mounted on the high metal gates. To avoid being recorded while in his alter ego, he held a large handkerchief to his face and blew his nose.

The gates opened as they approached and a woman – who Rafferty assumed, from the overalls and rubber gloves perched on the top of her basket, must be the cleaner – rode through on her bike. The taxi driver didn't wait for instructions but drove through.

New Hall's original structure, plain, basic, but sizeable, had stood foursquare to the elements for 250 years before its Victorian owner had added wings with arched windows and pargeting. They didn't fit comfortably with the simple fabric of the original. And even with the later extensions it could still scarcely be called a mansion as Caroline had implied; to Rafferty it appeared more a farmhouse with pretensions.

The grounds looked extensive. There was a large, empty forecourt with plenty of space for parking. A driveway at the side of the house led through a hedged opening. As Rafferty got out, he caught the flash of metal through the foliage as the evening sun glinted on parked cars. Above the roofline, tall poplars were visible behind the house.

He paid the driver and took a card so he could arrange a pick-up later. Always have your escape planned, he told himself as, with mixed feelings, he watched the cab head back up the drive towards the still-open gate. He wasn't sure what he expected from the evening. That bit in the advert about 'well-educated professionals' was beginning to play on his mind; perhaps he should have taken more notice of it? But he must have passed muster or Caroline Durward wouldn't have allowed him to sign up.

After he had passed a 'Parking' sign, which directed cars to park to the side of the house, he hesitated. He was nervous and had arrived early deliberately, preferring to walk into a room with few people than arrive late and be appraised by fifty or a hundred pairs of judgemental eyes. The front door was ajar. Assuming the guests were expected to just walk in, he did so, and followed the sound of classical music to the large drawing room. There were only two other people in the room: an urbane-looking man in his mid to late thirties and a young woman some ten years younger, with becomingly flushed cheeks and long, flowing, lustrous blonde hair. They were seated, chatting companionably on a settee, and failed to notice his arrival.

It was a large room, about thirty by forty feet, and divided by panelled folding doors in the centre which were currently folded back. A long run of old-fashioned French windows opened on to a flagged terrace that ran the length of the room. Although the intention had clearly been to cool the air, it was still oppressive. Rafferty loosened the collar of his new silk shirt, conscious he was sweating like a builder's labourer instead of perspiring lightly like the well-educated professional gentleman he purported to be. Every so often, in the distance, he could hear a clap of thunder, but it came no nearer and neither did any much-needed rain.

The interior of the room echoed the old-fashioned aspect provided by the French windows. It seemed stuck in a time-warp: all faded grandeur of worn, silk-covered sofas and amateur-looking watercolours. It didn't seem to match Caroline Durward's businesslike style. The sofas were placed either side of the almost baronial fireplace and more sofas lined the wall opposite the windows.

In the nearest corner Rafferty could just hear a grandfather clock solemnly tick away the seconds. It provided a tympanic accompaniment to the Bach or Mozart or whatever it was that was playing on the invisible sound system.

The other two people still hadn't noticed him and, tired of his department store mannequin take-off, Rafferty stepped forward into their line of vision. The pair broke off their conversation and stared at him. He wondered whether he should have knocked and waited outside. But he was here now and, after paying £500 for the privilege, he didn't see why he should stand on ceremony. But, like an owl hunting in daylight, he felt out of his element and he asked uncertainly, 'This *is* the venue for the Made in Heaven house party?'

The man's eyes narrowed momentarily,

swept him from head to toe as if he thought that Rafferty in his borrowed suit didn't quite cut the mustard, but then he smiled and said, 'Yes. That's right. Do come in and make yourself at home.' He nodded at the attractive young woman by his side. 'This is Jenny Warburton. She and I were just getting acquainted. I'm Guy Cranston, one of the partners in the agency.'

Jenny gave him a tentative, uncertain smile, which Rafferty returned before he introduced himself. 'Jo–Nigel Blythe.' Good start, Rafferty. Better go easy on the booze or God knows what else you'll nearly let slip.

'Nice to meet you, Nigel. Let me get you a drink. Wine all right? Red or white?'

Guy Cranston bustled over to a well-stocked sideboard with a concealed fridge at the far end of the room and brought Rafferty his wine. 'I'd better get the nibbles organised,' Cranston remarked as he headed back to the sideboard. Quickly, he laid out a dozen large dishes, emptied crisps and nuts and other assorted nibbles into them and then rejoined them.

Another half-dozen people arrived in a rush. Rafferty recognised Isobel, the agency receptionist, amongst them, though, as yet, there was no sign of Caroline Durward and Simon Farnell.

Isobel came over. 'Glad you could make it,' she said.

Although the welcoming comment was presumably meant for both him and Jenny, Rafferty couldn't help be aware that Isobel's smile was for him alone.

'Where's Caroline?' she asked Guy. 'It's not like her to be late for her own party.'

Guy shrugged, excused himself and moved over to greet the newcomers, leaving Rafferty and Jenny Warburton with Isobel.

Isobel laughed. 'Honestly, men! You'd think he'd have a clue as to his own wife's whereabouts.'

Beside him, Jenny, who seemed even more nervous than Rafferty, slopped her wine. Although she seemed embarrassed by her clumsiness it heartened Rafferty to think he wasn't alone in his nervous anticipation of the evening ahead.

Isobel sighed. 'I suppose that means that until Caroline gets here I'll have to act as hostess. I'll see you later,' she said and went to mingle.

Rafferty felt Jenny glance uncertainly at him. She seemed even more ill-at-ease now they had been left alone. She shot a look towards the door as if considering making a bolt for it. Rafferty felt an old-fashioned and chivalric instinct rise in his breast. Jenny was younger than him by about a decade, he guessed, and seemed shy. To head off the anticipated bolt and to clamp down on his own urge to do the same, he tried to put her at her ease. 'Have you been to many of these dating agency parties?' he asked. 'This is my first,' he admitted.

She gave him a strained smile. 'Funnily enough, it's my first, too.'

From her tone of voice, it sounded very much as if it might also be her last. Rafferty hoped not. 'I nearly chickened out,' he confided. As an ice-breaker, it wasn't exactly up there with the best one-liners of all time, but at least her smile, when it came, was wider this time. Rafferty felt things were improving, because her smile revealed delicious dimples in her cheeks. They matched the one in his chin. To his astonishment, she went on to gently tease him.

'You know what they say about faint hearts. But, having said that, I think I'll go.' She looked around the now crowded room as if searching for somewhere to put her untouched glass of wine. 'Somehow, I didn't expect such a crush.'

The smile quickly faded as if she felt intimidated by the occasion, the size of the room and the number of guests. Perhaps, like Rafferty, she was striving too hard for the cool sophistication of the other guests; the female ones at least, with their curiously expressionless faces, seemed cool to the point of catalepsy.

Rafferty, unwilling to be abandoned so soon, pleaded with her not to desert him.

'You're the only person I've had a chance to chat to. And seeing as we're both novices at this perhaps we should stick together.'

Her previous air of being ready to take flight slowly faded, though she still seemed ill-at-ease. After studying him for a few moments, she took a tentative sip of her wine, raised her chin a notch and said, 'Perhaps you're right. It would be cowardly to just run away.' She directed another dimpled smile at him. 'So, Nigel, tell me what made you join the agency?'

Rafferty shrugged. 'The usual reasons, I suppose. Never seem to meet anyone I click with and little time to look. Loneliness, too, I suppose,' he told her a little shamefacedly. 'What about you?'

'I suppose you could say I came here expecting to meet the man of my dreams.'

He tipped back the last of his wine, in his nervousness forgetting his earlier good intentions to go steady on the alcohol. 'What do you say I get us another drink, then you can tell me about your dream partner and I'll tell you about mine.'

She hesitated only a moment, then said, 'Why not? If you get the drinks I'll find us a couple of seats over there.' She nodded at a small alcove.

When Rafferty returned with the drinks he found Guy Cranston occupying the seat Jenny had kept for Rafferty. He had his arm round the back of her chair and, to Rafferty's irritation, looked set for the evening.

While at the bar, Rafferty had seen Caroline Durward and Simon Farnell arrive in a rush together, wearing matching expressions of annoyance. Seeing Rafferty, Caroline had come across to say hello and had ticked him off on her clipboard list. Now she was eyeing their little group frowningly from across the room. Rafferty guessed that, as one of the agency partners, Guy was expected to share the mingling and drawing-people-out duties, not home in on the girl that Rafferty considered the most attractive in the room.

From her expression, Jenny didn't welcome Guy's over-familiar attentions. Rafferty butted in and handed Jenny her wine. 'My seat, I think,' he said pointedly to Guy – damned if he was going to let him monopolise Jenny. He willed Guy to clear off.

Guy took the hint with reasonable grace. 'I'll leave you two to get better acquainted. Adieu, Jenny, till we meet again.'

Her 'Goodbye, Guy' was as pointed as Rafferty's.

Amazed, but delighted that Jenny should make clear she preferred *his* company to the far more suave and sophisticated-appearing Guy Cranston, Rafferty sat down. 'Persistent chap,' he said. 'Suppose you've got to expect a few like that at these affairs. Though you'd think, as a partner, he'd know better.'

‘Forget him,’ Jenny said firmly. ‘I intend to. Tell me about yourself. What do you do?’

Very soon, Rafferty found himself telling her his life history – or rather Jerry’s Nigel Blythe life story. She didn’t flinch when he revealed the estate agent bit. Though he couldn’t be entirely truthful given the many lies he had already told, he managed to slip in a few pieces of more personal information. He was surprised to find how much they had in common; they were both interested in history and architecture and, in spite of the age difference, they both liked the same music. They seemed to share similar ideas about a lot of things.

Their little alcove was in a corner, well tucked away from the main throng. More people had now arrived and the hubbub of talk rose as the drink went down; the cultured talk of the middle classes at play. He caught brief snatches of conversation – which, for all Rafferty knew to the contrary, sounded like knowledgeable references to Mahler and Leonard Bernstein, the latest books which had been well reviewed in the broadsheets, the latest play that was wowing them in the West End theatres. Rafferty, with only his fading knowledge of Sixties and Seventies pop music to help him keep his end up, would have felt out of it but for Jenny. They might have been quite alone. Rafferty found himself wishing they were.

Unfortunately, their little idyll was brought to an abrupt close as Simon Farnell swooped towards them. 'Now, now, what's this? We can't have you hiding yourselves away.' He gestured back towards the door. 'Caroline's sent me to tell you to mingle, dears. So come along.'

Simon took hold of Rafferty's arm in a vice-like grip and led him to a small mixed group. He introduced him and then left him to make conversation.

After a while, the conversation being the mix as before and above his head, Rafferty glanced round, looking for Jenny. He couldn't see her. Instead, his gaze was caught and held by Isobel, the agency receptionist. Isobel had removed the concealing wrap in which she had arrived. She was dressed to kill in a little black number; sleeveless, strapless and almost bodice-less, her bosom swelled out in lush, white curves. Few of the men could take their eyes off her, Rafferty included. She gave him a 'come hither' smile. Beside him, the man whom Simon Farnell had introduced as Dr Lancelot Bliss, the well-known TV Doctor, nudged Rafferty and murmured in his ear.

'Look but don't touch is the best advice there, old man. Isobel's determined to get some poor fool up the aisle – the richer the better. She's had her eye on Guy, but as he said, she's all right to bed, but not to wed.

Anyway, he wouldn't waste himself on Isobel even if he wasn't already married to Caroline, especially with the funds his late first wife left him.'

Rafferty was astonished to find himself the confidant of gossip; it seemed singularly inappropriate from a medical man, though the inappropriateness of his behaviour didn't seem to trouble the doctor. But then the well-known Bliss had presented his TV Doctor show for a number of years. No doubt mixing with the loveies, their behaviour had rubbed off.

Clearly, Dr Lancelot Bliss and loveiedom were as natural a pairing as rock stars and hard drugs. In creating his stir he held centre-stage; a place that was obviously his preferred location. Rafferty had already noticed the little attention-seeking gestures. Every minute or so, Bliss would let his thick, straight dark hair flop engagingly on to his forehead and just as regularly he swept it back. The gesture drew attention to both the shining thickness of the hair and the beauty of his hands, which were long, slender and artistic. His clothes were from the dressing-up box of the born show-off. The suit, though appearing plain at first glance, was a three-piece rather than a two-piece, the waistcoat and jacket silk-lined in a bright peacock blue at odds with the outward look of conservative sobriety. He even wore a fob-watch, an expensive bauble of exquisite beauty and workmanship.

Bliss broke into his thoughts. 'Isobel's father made several disastrous investments when she was around twelve and lost most of their money. Then, in the way of these things, the good money chased the bad. Guy Cranston let this out a few weeks ago after a few drinks too many.'

Rafferty was surprised. Guy Cranston didn't seem the type to turn garrulous with drink.

'Her mother persuaded Guy to offer her the agency job in the hope she'd snare a rich husband. So if you've got a few shekels, dear boy, take care. They're on the brink of losing the house – Latimer Court in Suffolk. Beautiful place, or it was – needs a fortune spending on it now. You've got to give it to Isobel. You'd never guess the family's problems from looking at her. She does rich very well.'

Rafferty said, 'Thanks for the tip. I'll steer well clear.'

Under his lashes, Rafferty let his gaze rest on Isobel, who was being very touchy-feely with a man of Mediterranean appearance. She threw back her head and laughed, displaying her long, white neck and rounded bosom to advantage. Isobel was dressed in what Rafferty presumed must be designer gear. And though there wasn't much of it, the scrap of material was clearly not off-the-peg and had presumably cost as much as his borrowed and ill-fitting suit. Diamonds glittered at her ears and throat. If she was wearing the last of her family's money as an 'investment' she hid it well. Rafferty would never have guessed her to be desperate. In spite of the indiscretion about Darius's little drugs business that Rafferty remembered, it seemed Isobel could be discreet when it mattered to her.

'As I said, Guy only gave her the job as a favour to her mother; he knew the family through his late wife. Though I think Guy's rather regretting it now. He says Isobel's becoming a pest, always ringing him, telling him she loves him. She's set her cap there all right.'

Between all the introductions, the wine and Lancelot Bliss's gossip, Rafferty lost the thread, forgot he was meant to be a smooth, sophisticated, urban professional, and blurted out, 'But I thought you said he was married to Caroline?'

Lancelot stared at him as if astonished that his confidant should have turned out to be a naive provincial. 'Usual thing, Nigel,' he explained with a patronising air that was reminiscent of Rafferty's cousin. 'Caro and Guy have what you might call a semi-detached marriage. It seems to work okay for them. But keep it under your hat. It wouldn't do for it to get out, not in *their* line of work. Some clients might feel let down. It's what made Isobel think she might be in with a chance of turning Guy from semi-detached to detached and available.'

Rafferty raised what he hoped was a sophisticated eyebrow to enquire, 'And how did Caroline take that?'

'Didn't turn a hair of that immaculately groomed head, though I believe Isobel has since felt the nip of Jack Frost. Caroline keeps Guy on a long leash and lets him roam. That way he always comes back. Caro knows her man. Guy loves 'em and leaves 'em. But I imagine he finds marriage to Caroline way too convenient to leave *her*. It keeps him safe from the predatory Isobels of this world, do you see?'

Rafferty did see, though the seeing deflated him a little. If Lancelot Bliss was to be believed, the agency wasn't immune from the lying, cheating and betrayal so prevalent elsewhere. Perhaps he'd wasted his money paying for what was already so freely available. But then he remembered Jenny Warburton. The memory gave him a warm glow that had nothing to do with the sultry weather.

'Poor Isobel, one has to feel rather sorry for her. Because she has not only that costly designer outfit on her back, she's got her family perched there as well.' Lancelot plucked another glass of wine – his sixth by Rafferty's counting – from a passing waiter and knocked half of it back. It served to make him even more garrulous. 'So if Isobel finally gets the message that Guy's giving her, she'll be man-hunting elsewhere with even more desperation.'

From Rafferty's other side, a man he recalled being introduced as Ralph Dryden commented, 'Poor girl's deluded. Didn't you say her father suffered from a similar affliction, Lance?'

Bliss nodded. 'Runs in the family, according to Guy. He told me her father's convinced he's the next Richard Branson. Considering he apparently gets involved in one idiotic money-*losing* scheme after another, his delusions must be of the certifiable variety.' He looked at Ralph and added, 'Still, we all know what they say about a fool and his money.' For some reason this comment caused Ralph Dryden's plump face to flush hotly.

Whether Ralph had become unwisely entangled with Isobel, Rafferty didn't know. But of one thing he was sure – dressed as she was, Isobel looked no man's idea of a suitable girl to take home to mother, never mind marry. She looked strictly mistress material. Jenny, on the other hand, although, like Caroline and a number of the other women, dressed in a sleeveless little black number with a hint of cleavage, still managed to give off a demure air. It had appealed to him from the moment he had met her.

Lancelot Bliss must have exhausted his gossip for he fell silent. Now Ralph Dryden drawled loudly in Rafferty's other ear.

'So what is it you do, anyway, Nigel?'

'Property,' Rafferty answered as briefly as politeness permitted. But his interrogator probed further.

'What area? Only I'm in a similar line myself. My firm designed and built Elmhurst Heights, the new apartment development by the docks.'

An unfortunate coincidence, as Elmhurst Heights was the apartment block Rafferty's cousin, Nigel, lived in. With its futuristic concrete and metal design it was the sort of modern development Rafferty most loathed. He was wondering whether some sort of compliment was expected and was still trying to come up with one that sounded vaguely sincere when Dryden saved him the trouble.

'It's featured in most of the top architectural journals, both in this country and abroad,' he boasted. 'Rory here did a rather good TV piece on it.'

Ralph droned loudly on. Rafferty succeeded in tuning him out until Ralph remembered his earlier question and, in the roar necessary to be heard above the music and assorted drink-fuelled conversations, he reminded him, 'But you still haven't said what exactly it is that you do.'

'I'm an estate agent,' Rafferty roared reluctantly back into a sudden lull in both music and conversation. A number of heads turned in his direction and scrutinised him. The revelation brought several seconds' more silence. He looked round the circle of faces: boastful Ralph Dryden, Property Developer Man; Rory Gifford, the dark, thrown-together, Bohemian-looking TV producer friend of Lancelot Bliss who he had learned produced Lance's TV programme; Adam Ardley, the website designer; Toby Rufford-Lyle, the London barrister; the lowering-browed Tony Something who worked 'in the City'. Even Lance, the gossipy TV Doctor, seemed to have run out of chat.

To be fair, perhaps, as he had, their little group had all experienced estate agents' more underhand tricks. Sensing the group was itching to top each other's buying and selling horror stories which his presence prevented, he said, 'Excuse me, must do some more mingling,' and took himself off to the other side of the room from where he was amused to see their discussion became animated. He caught several glances and knew they wouldn't forget him in a hurry.

Simon Farnell appeared at his elbow. 'All alone, dear?' he asked. 'Let me introduce you to some other people.' Before he could drag him off to another group, Rafferty said, 'I thought I'd get another drink first.'

'Dutch courage, is it? Go on then.' Like the mother hen to which Caroline Durward had likened him, Simon shooed him off towards the bar, then hurried to catch him up, to whisper, 'By the way, dear, the accent's slip-ping.'

As he stood at the bar, he studied the women covertly; as he reminded himself, finding a partner *was* the reason he had come. Though, apart from Jenny, none of the other women appealed to him. All were discreetly made up and attractive in an understated way, but to Rafferty they all looked alike. Mostly blondes in little black numbers that contrasted so well with the perfect skin and shiny hair. Their bosoms, too, seemed to come in regulation sizes; Isobel aside, none were too voluptuous or too meagre. Even their voices sounded similar, well modulated, nothing too strident. Caroline Durward, although a good ten years older, shared the blonde, unlined, well-groomed look. It occurred to him that he could be attending a plastic surgeons' convention where the greatest successes were paraded. Briefly, Rafferty wondered where the failures were stored. Up in the attic, presumably, where, like Dorian Grey, they could do their time-withered bit out of sight. Rafferty preferred the more natural beauty of Jenny Warburton.

As people and conversations moved around him, he learned that most had names that ended in the upmarket 'a' sound. It accorded with his theory that the names of the common herd tended to end in an 'i' sound, such as Kylie, Shelley, Tracey, Tiffany, Kimberley, Tammy, Billie and so on, and mostly applied more to girls. Upmarket names ended in an 'a' sound, such as Lucinda, Lydia, Fiona, Diana, Miranda, Emma and Amanda and the really posh ones followed no rules at all – just like the more free-spirited of the working classes. Both often still gave their kids biblical, classical, historical or royal names, such as Adam, Anne, Andrew, Elizabeth, Matthew, Luke, Mark, John, Charles, Edward, George and William as opposed to the designer-gear-wearing, celebrity-aping working class, who favoured names such as Kylie and the like.

Was it a coincidence, Rafferty wondered, that his cousins Jerry and Terry shared the downmarket 'i' sound? At least, as a *Joseph*, I'm as biblical as the aristos, he was able to comfort himself, until he realised his theory fell down because Jerry was actually Jeremiah, which put him in the upmarket name area.

Of course, being his theory, it fell far short of proof. No doubt, if he mentioned it to

Llewellyn, he would soon put him straight on it much as he did with most of his too-ready murder theories as to who had dunnit.

Two hours later Rafferty decided he'd done more than enough mingling and sought out Jenny again. He glimpsed her through the crowd. She wore a glazed look as some man with a supercilious expression shouted in her ear above the noise. Rafferty, about to butt in, was saved the trouble, as she put down her empty glass, said a few quiet goodbyes and made for the door.

As he edged his way after Jenny, Rafferty noticed Isobel Goddard slip out the door behind her. Before he followed them, Rafferty glanced over his shoulder, wanting to be sure no more demands to mingle threatened. He couldn't spot any of the agency partners in the now-heaving room and guessed they were taking a well-earned break. They had worked hard and had successfully retrieved shrinking violets from the terrace throughout the evening. Rafferty had several times found himself numbered amongst those so retrieved.

Relieved to have evaded another such retrieval, Rafferty firmly closed the drawing-room door behind him, enclosing its babble of conversation. As his feet clicked on the marble-tiled entrance hall Isobel glanced behind her, before she headed off towards the Ladies'.

Rafferty caught up with Jenny by the front door. 'You didn't say goodbye,' he told her. Teasingly, he added, 'To me or Guy.'

'I'm sorry. I did look for you earlier. I was hoping you'd rescue me from that awful man. And I've already said goodbye to Guy Cranston. I must go. Though I don't normally work Saturdays I've got to go in early tomorrow and do a few hours. I didn't intend to stay out so late.'

'Nor me.' With Dafyd Llewellyn on honeymoon, Rafferty had been forced to look after his own paperwork; most of it was still awaiting his attention. He had intended to stay only an hour or so and weigh up whether he was wasting his time, his money and his cousin's expensive suit. As he had expected, the rest of the members were way out of his normal social orbit. Jenny, though, seemed different, sweet and down-to-earth. There was something vulnerable about her which he found very appealing.

Now full of the previously spurned Dutch courage, Rafferty said, 'I'd like to see you again. May I ring you?' Shame Llewellyn couldn't hear that grammatical 'may', he reflected.

Jenny glanced up at him and smiled. 'I'd like that. Have you got a pen?'

Rafferty had – he'd come armed with three and two small notebooks just in case.

Jenny quickly scribbled her telephone

number down, adding as she did so, 'I'll be home around 10.30 tomorrow and will be in for the rest of the day.'

Pleased, Rafferty nodded and took out Nigel's mobile. 'Better ring for a cab. Can I get one for you? Or we could share?' he suggested hopefully.

'I've got my car, thanks. I only had two small glasses of wine so should be under the limit.'

Two of the other guests came out of the toilet allocated to the men, glanced at Rafferty and Jenny where they stood by the front door, and headed slowly back to the drawing room.

'Didn't you say you live near the docks? It's on my way. I'll drop you if you like.'

Rafferty would have liked – very much. But he had given her Nigel's address earlier. He rather regretted it now. If he and Jenny became an item he'd have to stage a swift house move to his real address. And a swift name change, too, he reminded himself. It was a pity that when he had arranged to borrow his cousin's identity he had thought no further than the concealment of his actions from his ma. He hoped Jenny was the understanding sort she seemed to be.

But for now, he couldn't take the chance that Jenny might say yes to the expected 'come up for coffee, etc' scenario. While he might have a key to Nigel's apartment, he doubted, even if he could find them, that he would master Nigel's coffee-making gadgets. He sensed Jenny might be special and he didn't want to look a fool. Anyway, he had her phone number. He would ask her out for a meal and begin to woo her properly. Besides, he discovered he was busting for a pee; very romantic.

By now, they found themselves outside the front door. Rafferty made the excuse he was meeting friends later and was heading in the opposite direction. After Jenny gave him a quick peck on the cheek, Rafferty stood on the top step feeling ridiculously happy and watched Jenny walk away. She turned and waved at him before she reached the side of the house where the cars were parked and disappeared from view.

The scent of Jenny's perfume hung in the still air and his nostrils flared as he breathed it in. But nature prevented his own 'I have been here before', Rossetti moment, as he recalled Llewellyn had once described a similar occasion. He had to rush back inside.

As he made for the Gents' lavatory, he could hear the gurgling of ancient plumbing echoing through the slightly open door of the Ladies' toilet. It almost drowned the still-rising crescendo of talk and laughter heard through the thickly panelled door of the large drawing room.

Half anxious that one of the agency staff

might yet appear and collar him again, Rafferty hurried into the Gents'. It was empty. He relieved himself, washed his hands, then took out Nigel's mobile. The power was getting low, he noticed. Nigel hadn't bothered to put it on charge. He made a mental note to put his own phone and Nigel's on charge when he got home.

As he rang for the cab, he studied the slip of paper with Jenny's number on it and grinned inanely. But the grin faded as he remembered the gates were controlled electronically. Good manners required him to say his goodbyes, but he felt reluctant to re-enter the fray. He'd get the cabbie to ring through so he could leave. Jenny hadn't returned so she must have managed to get out.

Rafferty left and walked up the drive to await his cab. He had only to wait five minutes before the cab pulled up. After he explained to the cab driver and got him to speak into the intercom, the gates opened and Rafferty slipped through.

With a contented sigh, he settled himself in the rear seat, glad to sit back in the quiet of the cab and just dream.

Three

It was Saturday lunchtime. Rafferty frowned and replaced the receiver as Jenny Warburton's ansafone picked up for the third time in as many hours. He had left a message each time, but Jenny hadn't returned his calls even though she'd told him only yesterday that she would be at home from 10.30 onwards.

As he pushed out of the public phone box – having forgotten to charge up either his mobile or the one Nigel had given him – Rafferty reflected sadly on the changing fates. At one time – and not so long ago either – he had only to pick up his so-called 'little black book' and he'd have an amusing companion for the evening and often a satisfying partner for the night as well. A gift from his ma, his little black book was actually sky-blue with a rainbow arching over both front and back covers. But suddenly, his little not-black book was filled with more crossings-out than entries, the terse explanations through the cancellation lines said: married; seriously dating; moved to Newcastle; emigrated. Emigrated! Talk about the ultimate brush-off.

Though, if he was honest, he had been the one whose previous lack of willingness to commit had helped to bring about those marriages, those steady relationships, those upping of sticks to Newcastle or Sydney. He'd had no lack of 'willing to commit' ladies to complain about as his ma had frequently pointed out to him.

He decided he deserved the consolation of a swift half of Adnams and popped into the nearest pub. But before he ordered the beer, he visited the Gents' and after using the facilities, he disconsolately studied his face in the mirror. He saw blue eyes that had been a more intense blue in his youth, the thick mop of unruly auburn hair and the chin with the dimple. Not wildly handsome, not even his ma would say that, but he wasn't plug-ugly, either. He was an average-looking bloke, with all his own teeth. So what was wrong with him that had decided Jenny not to answer his calls?

It couldn't be his looks. Average-looking – and worse – men found women to love them. Perhaps it was his manner? Hadn't Llewellyn implied he had a tendency to be too glib and jokey? It was a protective skin, of course. What he needed to do, and he didn't know if he was capable of it, was to try to shed at least some of his protective skin and dare to bare the inner man, the deeper, more spiritual side. Trouble was, he was worried he might discover he didn't *have* a more spiritual side. Like the child who actually *met* the bogeyman, he feared the early Catholic indoctrination had driven any spirituality so far underground he'd need an earth-mover to disinter it.

His earlier relationships had been superficial and ultimately unsatisfying; much like his marriage to Angie, his late wife. It had only been Llewellyn's steady and serious courtship of his cousin Maureen that had brought home to him that lasting relationships were not necessarily to be found between the pages of a little black book; not even if it was the blue of a summer sky with a hopeful but meteorologically unlikely rainbow arching over all.

But as he left the Gents' and his soul-searching behind him and ordered his beer, Rafferty consoled himself with the thought that he'd taken a step in the right direction; even if, with Jenny, that step had turned out to be a false one, he'd done something positive to help himself and that must surely be a good thing.

He found a table and sat down. After he had swallowed half his drink, he forced himself to accept that Jenny had changed her mind and didn't want to see him again. But it still upset him. He had taken to Jenny at once and had thought she had liked him, too. Disappointed, Rafferty put thoughts of Jenny from his mind. Plenty more fish in the Made In Heaven sea, he told himself even as the plaintive little voice remarked that, for him, not one of them had held the same appeal as Jenny. But even though Jenny didn't want him, someone else might, and after paying out so much money for the privilege of attending their parties, he was damned if he was going to just throw it all away. He should just stick with it and wait for the different occasions to come round. He finished his beer and headed for home.

As he picked up his car keys that evening and set off for town, Rafferty reflected that it was fortunate the agency social whirl left little time for brooding. The party tonight was to be held in the annexe of The Elmhurst, the posh hotel on Northgate. Close to the centre of town, it was one of Elmhurst's larger hotels.

Rafferty had been in The Elmhurst before – the bar, anyway – but never its annexe. For some reason, he had been expecting some kind of cobbled-together construction. The word 'annexe' to him always suggested 'making do' Fifties austerity. But after he had parked his car a discreet distance away, shown his invitation to the two smartly uniformed doormen and followed the signs for the Made In Heaven party, he saw there was no sense of making do at *this* annexe. Stupid, really, that he had imagined there might be.

The Elmhurst was a four-star hotel with everything provided for its guests' comfort. And although not particularly old – being no earlier than Edwardian – The Elmhurst was opulent, from the gorgeously decorated ceiling in the largest of the three ballrooms to the deep marble baths and even deeper mattresses on the huge double beds in the suites that Rafferty had only heard about. But then those years before the First World War were golden ones for the wealthy.

As he entered the second of the hotel's annexe ballrooms and glanced round, the opulence made him feel even more conscious that he was wearing Nigel's peacock suit for the third time in a week. He had convinced himself that members who had attended both parties must know the suit almost as well as he did. The silk shirt was the same also, though he had washed it himself first thing that morning. Perhaps it was time he splashed out.

Mentally, Rafferty reviewed his tired wardrobe and knew, if he was going to continue attending the social functions of the Made In Heaven agency, he'd have to get himself suitably kitted out. He couldn't expect to make a long-term loan out of Nigel's suit.

'Clothes maketh the man' had never been Rafferty's watchword phrase as it seemed to be Llewellyn's. But if he wanted his membership of the agency to achieve the desired result he would have to accept he would be judged on his appearance. And whether he liked it or not clothes were part of that outward show.

He decided, a little later, as he grabbed his second glass of wine from a passing waiter and met and held the encouraging gaze of an engagingly monkey-faced young woman standing some six yards away, that he could get to like such an extravagant lifestyle. Emboldened by her encouraging smile, Rafferty made his way towards her, snaffling another glass of wine on the way so he had something to offer besides himself.

She smiled. 'Just what I like; a man who can command the attention of waiters.'

Her face looked even more endearingly monkey-cute at close quarters, he realised as he handed her the glass. 'That's me,' said Rafferty. 'Elmhurst's very own Michael Winner.'

'Don't tell me you're a film director, too?'

Briefly tempted, Rafferty decided not to go down that road. He'd already told enough lies. 'No. The only directing I do is of people around bijoux residences I think they might want to buy.' *Bijoux residences* – God, Rafferty, you're getting a bit too into this estate-agent speak, he told himself. Before you know it, you'll be talking like Nigel, who was all 'select apartments', never 'flats', and 'spaciously laid-out' instead of 'barn-like and expensive to heat'.

'Pity, because I'm an actress. At least, that's what I do when I'm not "resting" – doing temp jobs of typing and filing for bosses who work you to death and who think their pay entitles them to groping privileges. Damn.' Her face fell. 'I forgot I'd intended to be all sophisticated. And me an actress, too.'

Rafferty grinned. 'We can always try "let's pretend".'

'What do you mean?'

'Let's pretend we've just met and start again. I'm Nigel, by the way. Nigel Blythe.' Rafferty was beginning to realise how much he hated the name. Why couldn't Jerry have chosen a name with a bit more dash to it? Adam, he could cope with, or even Sebastian, which had a touch of the *droit de seigneurs* about it.

'I'm Estelle Meredith.'

'So, Estelle, you're an actress. You've done all the classical roles, I take it? Ophelia, Desdemona, Lady Macbeth?' Thankfully, as that was the limit of Rafferty's knowledge of classical female leads, Estelle broke in.

'God, yes. You name it, I've played it. You should have seen my Portia. I weighed the quality of mercy and served it up in such a neat parcel I got three standing ovations. That was a month ago, but I can still feel the tingle. Hollywood is mad for me. I'm to fly out next week to try out for several leading roles.'

'No.' Rafferty's face fell.

'No's right.' Estelle's face went into matching freefall. 'We're playing let's pretend, remember? Unfortunately, next week I'm back in a lowly role in a temporary production of Grabbit and Robbem, set in a firm of solicitors. Likely to be a limited production as Grabbit is only too prone to do just that. Should be paid danger money.'

'Failing that,' said Rafferty, as he magicked another couple of glasses of wine from a disappearing waiter, 'how about a little bit of anaesthesia?'

'Cheers. Anyway, enough about me. Tell me about you, Nigel. I suppose you have to do a certain amount of acting in your line?'

'Oh yes. That's certainly true.' The funny thing was that even as he became better at play-acting, he felt increasingly loathe to do it, especially when, like now, he liked someone.

'It's all lies, anyway, isn't it?'

Rafferty stared at her. Had he been sussed?

'Acting, I mean,' Estelle enlarged.

'I suppose it is' was Rafferty's lame reply. 'Can I get you some nibbles before they all go?'

'Please. I'm starved. I had a late audition today and didn't have time to eat before I left to come here. They want to see me again. I've a chance, a real chance, this time. I feel sure of it. And it would be a terrific role, really challenging. It's a good company, too, and the play seems likely to have a long run in the West End. I'm sure I can do it. All I need is the chance.'

'Tell me about it,' Rafferty invited.

For a moment, Estelle hesitated, as if worried that to speak about a dream would make it go pop. But then, encouraged by Rafferty's genuine interest, shining-eyed and breathless with hope, she *did* tell him. She explained the role and what it would mean to her. Before she'd got to the end of her explanation, they somehow found themselves squashed together in a corner behind an enormous floral display, their game of 'let's pretend' completely forgotten as they found they both preferred the reality of each other – or the near-reality in Rafferty's case.

Estelle Meredith's engaging, monkey face grew even more appealing to Rafferty as the evening wore on. As he gazed into her golden, toffee-apple coloured eyes he felt the urge to stroke the wild tangle of fair hair that cascaded around her shoulders. But then he remembered her earlier remark about gropers and restrained the urge. She was harder-edged than Jenny Warburton, and had a mischievous, dare-anything air. It intrigued Rafferty so much that he had ignored Simon Farnell's repeated appeals to mingle and remained by her side for the evening.

To his annoyance, Guy Cranston had once again tried to muscle in – it seemed they shared similar tastes in women – but this time, Rafferty hadn't been forced to ease him out. Although Estelle had chatted pleasantly enough to both of them for five minutes, at the end of that time she had managed to convey to Guy that his presence was no longer required. To Rafferty's relief, although he looked a bit crestfallen, Guy immediately took himself off.

The evening ended all too soon for Rafferty. Too late, he realised he had been so smitten by Estelle that he had swallowed wine like water. If he hadn't, he could have offered to drive her home. But even in his current, alcohol-influenced rosy glow, something wiser than himself warned him not to court the attention of the traffic cops when he was being Nigel.

He sensed that Estelle could be important to him, important to his future. He knew he'd have to sort out the little discrepancy of his altered identity some time, just not yet. Certainly not with a traffic cop breathing in his alcohol fumes while he demanded his name and papers.

It was getting on for midnight, already people were leaving. But Rafferty and Estelle deliberately lengthened the evening's enchantment by going out through the open door at the back of the annexe and into the grounds for a breath of fresh air. They exchanged phone numbers seated on a convenient bench beneath the stars.

It was unfortunate that just as Estelle was showing a ready willingness to be kissed, his mobile went off. But at least he managed to pull the correct one from his pocket. It was the station. They wanted him in. Rafferty knew he had no choice but to make his excuses to Estelle.

He left the annexe by the side entrance to avoid getting delayed by the loud and lengthy 'good nights' of his fellow members and was halfway to the station when his mobile went again. It was the station with an 'as you were' message. The problem that had required his presence had been resolved.

Rafferty sighed and almost as soon as he wondered whether he should head back to the party he decided against it. Even if Estelle hadn't left by now, he feared to somehow endanger the happy glow brought by their sweet parting if he attempted to revisit it. So he hailed a cab and as he climbed in the back and it set off for his flat, he gave himself up to dreaming.

Strange, he thought, that he should have spent so many years not even coming close to falling in love and then should fall for two different girls one after the other. The memory of Jenny's deliberate brush-off sobered him. He felt sure that wouldn't happen again. Estelle, as an actress, was only too well acquainted with the pain of rejection. He was certain she would die before she did such a thing.

Rafferty had met Estelle on the Saturday and it wasn't till the Monday morning that he had learned from Bill Beard the horrifying news that Estelle had been found murdered in the grounds of The Elmhurst's annexe.

What had he said to himself? That Estelle would die before she gave him the distant brush-off? And she had died.

It seemed to be the season for bad news, for more arrived the following morning when Rafferty, hanging about the canteen to keep tabs on how Harry Simpson's investigation into Estelle's murder was progressing, discovered just why Jenny hadn't responded to his phone calls.

Her car had never left the grounds of the Cranstons' home. And even as he struggled to come up with a non-sinister explanation as to why this should be, Rafferty knew he was only fooling himself. It was too much of a coincidence that Jenny's car should have been discovered still parked at the house, a few yards from where a young woman's brutally battered body had been found concealed behind New Hall's large rubbish bins by the council's refuse collectors.

Although he shied away from the thought, Rafferty knew he had to face the appalling probability that the body was Jenny's and with it came the realisation that she must have been there since Friday, the night of the first party, the night he had so cheerfully waved her off to her murderer.

Four

Rafferty was beginning to fear he must be a jinx where women were concerned. His wife had died young – murdered by cancer. But although that hadn't been love – only lust, a faulty Durex and a pregnancy that had miscarried only after they had made their hasty marriage – Rafferty felt a pattern was forming.

His wife had died young, Estelle had died young. Now, so had Jenny Warburton. Lonely old age stared him in the face. For certain it was that he dare not risk falling in love again...

According to DI Harry Simpson, who had been assigned both murders, Estelle and Jenny had been brutally hacked and bludgeoned, though unusually, Jenny's murder, clearly the first, was a more violent affair than Estelle's. If they were the victims of a serial killer as Harry confided was his suspicion, it would have been more normal – if you could use such a word in relation to such appalling *ab*normality – for the second victim, Estelle, to have suffered the usual escalation in violence.

Yet, such wasn't the case according to Harry, when, looking like death himself, the DI had returned to the station. It was then, between hacking coughs, that he had repeated Bill Beard's comment which, although he had been expecting it, had chilled Rafferty's blood all over again.

'Luckily, we've got a prime suspect already.' *Cough, cough, cough*. 'Chap called Nigel Blythe's in the frame for both murders.' Harry coughed again, seized a strangled breath and went on. 'Turns out he was definitely the last to see both girls, that is, if the body which has just been discovered does turn out to be the owner of the red hatchback parked at the house.'

'Didn't the Cranstons think it odd that one of their members' cars should have been abandoned in their grounds?'

'I wondered about that. But it seems the guests, particularly if they've drunk too much to drive, often leave their cars at the house for several days at a time, especially when urgent business calls them away without the chance to retrieve their vehicles.

'According to witnesses, this Nigel Blythe left both the agency parties on successive nights with one or other girl in tow. He was last seen exiting the rear door of The Elmhurst's annexe with Estelle Meredith. As you know, her body was found behind some bushes in the grounds.' Harry paused, found another wheezing breath and continued. 'Several of the party guests told me there was something not quite right about this Nigel Blythe.'

'Not quite right?' Rafferty repeated before he clutched at the proverbial straw. 'Reliable witnesses, you reckon?' As expected, the straw immediately bent.

'Seem to be. They're all singing from the same hymn sheet, anyway, and they were interviewed separately. Unsurprisingly, this Blythe seems to have done a bunk. He's not at his flat. Place has been ransacked, too.' Harry gave him a strange look. 'You've gone a queer colour, Rafferty. Someone walked over your grave?'

'Something like that,' Rafferty muttered, before he slinked off back to his office. Harry Simpson was a fine one to comment about *my* queer colour, Rafferty thought. Simpson had been going about the station like an omen of death for months. The weight had fallen off him. Although Harry's insistence to everybody who asked was that he had been on a strict diet, this was patently not the case. Somehow, Harry had found the strength to carry on. But it was obvious it couldn't last. He was clearly suffering and looked weighted down by this horrific double murder. It couldn't be long before he had to bow to his body's demands and take sick leave.

Rafferty's gaze alighted on the skinned-over cup of cold tea on his desk and he frowned. He couldn't remember getting it. In fact, lately, there had been a few things he couldn't remember doing – like buying the food that had suddenly appeared in his fridge. But these mysteries were edged out of his mind by other, more important considerations, like the fact he was now doubly in the frame for murder. He'd liked Jenny and Estelle a lot and had agonised as to whether he should come clean. But how could he do so now? It might have been a different matter if he had done so after the discovery of Estelle's body when her identity had been confirmed. But now?

That first, instinctive denial that he knew Estelle had forced him to tangle himself in so many more lies that now he was so hopelessly compromised no one would believe in his innocence.

He'd thought at first that if – when – Harry Simpson went on sick leave and he was put in charge of the investigation, for him – and the victims – it would be a *good thing.* Rafferty knew he hadn't murdered anybody, so, unlike Harry, he could concentrate on finding who *had.* But, of course, with him, things were never that simple. Because once he'd thought about it, he realised with what difficulties being in charge of the case would present him. For a start, even with the alterations to his appearance he had already decided were necessary, coming face-to-face with the witnesses was going to be a nerve-racking business, spent waiting for one or more to point the finger and say, 'But that's *him*. That's Nigel Blythe. The *murderer*.'

He'd already begun to give nervous starts whenever Nigel's name was mentioned. Even Ma was becoming concerned about his strange behaviour and had suggested he go to the doctor and get a tonic for his nerves.

Certainly, keeping a low profile when you're meant to be fronting a major enquiry was going to be a tall order. On the other hand, as the officer in charge, he would be nicely placed to steer the investigation away from his innocent cousin and himself and aim it at whoever the real killer might be.

It was fortunate that he had shown an unusual prescience in drinking at an unfamiliar pub and using a strange cab firm to take him to the first party. It meant no one would be able to give a description of his car or reveal his real identity. Even better – from his point of view, rather than Jerry's – he had decided to get into his Nigel Blythe role before the party and had ordered the cab in his cousin's name – though that had of course brought its own problems.

The inevitable discovery that someone had

masqueraded as Nigel while the real Nigel had been far away in York at the time of the two murders would also serve to delay the investigation, though Rafferty feared it could only be a matter of time before someone thought to backtrack from the real Nigel to his friends, acquaintances and family – and found *him*.

There was no way he could impede the investigation into 'Nigel', who, as Harry had soon discovered, had shown such a particular interest in the two victims; it would only draw unwanted attention to him. But as he didn't want his cousin to remain in the frame for longer than necessary, before Harry Simpson and his team discovered that Estelle had supposedly left the party in The Elmhurst with 'Nigel Blythe', Rafferty had set his other little deception in motion. He had felt he had no choice about arranging the hastily improvised burglary at Nigel's apartment; if he hadn't his cousin would have squealed at the first opportunity. As it was, convincing his cousin to keep silent had been a close-run thing.

It was fortunate that Harry Simpson had decided – until Nigel Blythe could be traced and interviewed – to keep his name under wraps. It was the reason his cousin had agreed, albeit under protest, that as he couldn't even officially *know* about the murders, he would keep quiet for the time being. After all, as Rafferty had pointed out to him, he had an alibi and would soon exonerate himself once his whereabouts had been officially traced. But if Jerry, under pressure, decided to come clean, what was *he* to say?

Rafferty thanked his guardian angel that Jerry had been miles away in York at the times of both murders and would, as he had claimed, be able to provide solid alibis for both.

Jerry hadn't reckoned on getting involved in a double murder enquiry when he handed over his ID for a 'lark' and two hundred smackers. Neither had Rafferty, but at least, unlike Jerry, he expected shortly to be in a position to attempt to guide events.

Guilt and unwillingness to expose his guilt to his cousin's sharp-tongued fury had encouraged Rafferty to put off ringing him. But aware it was likely to be only a matter of time before Harry Simpson discovered Jerry's whereabouts, Rafferty knew he had to get in first and fess up to his cousin before Jerry blurted out his involvement. And when Rafferty had finally plucked up the courage to confess to Jerry that he had unwittingly been put in the frame for murder, Jerry, not unnaturally, had been as livid as Rafferty had feared.

'You said there'd be no grief. Nothing dicey

you said—'

'I know what I said,' Rafferty had told him. 'But be fair – how was I to know some murdering madman would join the dating agency? I know I've landed you in the shit and—'

'Damn right you have. And if it wasn't for the fact that my love life's a thousand times more successful than yours and gives me a rock solid alibi for Saturday night I'd be in it up to my neck. It's no thanks to you that I'm not.'

Rafferty supposed he should be grateful that Jerry's boasts about his love life were not idle ones and provided him with a solid alibi from an unimpeachable if undoubtedly slightly promiscuous source.

'Look, my colleagues may not realise it yet, but believe me, you're out of it,' Rafferty assured him. 'I'm the one in it up to the neck.' He ignored Jerry's muttered 'good' and added, 'But even though you've got an alibi for Saturday, the night of Estelle Meredith's murder, I lost no time in setting up a scenario that leaves strong doubts that you even joined the dating agency.'

'I *didn't*,' Jerry forcefully reminded him. 'That was you. Remember?'

Rafferty did, only too clearly.

'Anyway, tell me about this so-called brainwave of yours that'll convince your colleagues I had no involvement. Though, to be brutally frank, dear boy, the thought of a brainwave from one of the Rafferty side of the family does little to inspire confidence.'

'I staged a little burglary at your flat.'

'*Apartment.* It's an apartment, not the dingy council accommodation the word *flat* brings to mind,' Jerry, the estate agent, had automatically insisted, before it dawned on him what Rafferty had said. 'You did what? If you've broken anything, I'll—'

Rafferty had interrupted before Jerry got into his stride. 'Calm down. Nothing's broken. But don't you see, this way, the use of your credit card and passport is easily explained. And the layout of those flats – *apartments*,' he quickly corrected himself, 'was designed for maximum privacy which means that no casual visitor to the other apartments would be likely to notice the door to yours was ajar or tell how long it had been that way. And they didn't. I checked.'

Rafferty had made sure he kept within sniffing distance of the case from the time Estelle's identity was established and knew almost as much about it as Harry Simpson. Harry had been unable to find anyone who knew anything about the burglary or when it had occurred, apart from Rafferty's other cousin, the obliging Terry Tierney, who had reported it. As far as Harry Simpson and his team knew – or would know as soon as they officially traced Nigel to York – the apartment had been broken into the night Nigel had left for his estate agents' convention by someone who had watched him load his bags into his car boot in the parking bay that had thoughtfully been allocated the same number as his apartment.

Rafferty, not wishing another of his cousins to have a hold on him, had told Terry he hadn't reported the burglary because he wanted to avoid the paperwork. Thankfully, Terry, aware of Rafferty's aversion to pen-pushing, had swallowed his excuse and agreed, for a consideration, to 'discover' the burglary for him.

'I've arranged for Terry Tierney to ring you with the bad news,' he had told Jerry, 'just to cover our backs. It will be natural for you to rush home and go through the motions of checking what's been "stolen".'

'Just make sure that nothing else goes missing in the meantime. It'll be down to you if it does. I've got a lot of expensive gear in that apartment and—'

'It won't.'

'Oh yeah?' Jerry sneered. 'And how did you explain that? A burglar who doesn't like top-of-the-range electrical gadgets? It's not very likely.'

'A lot of burglars are opportunistic. They'll take credit cards, money, passports and other portable stuff that can be easily sold on. And another thing,' Rafferty had added as he thought on the hoof. 'Don't forget you'll have to query the bill from the Made In Heaven dating agency on your credit card statement, as it'll be a large one. And cancel the card.'

At this reminder of the additional trouble to which he'd be put, Jerry cursed Rafferty. 'This is the last time I do you a favour,' he hissed down the phone. 'As if it's not enough that I'm now the chief suspect in a murder enquiry I'm going to have the grief of replacing my passport as well. Not to mention having hassle with the credit card company. They're sure to think I'm pulling a fast one to get out of paying their huge bill.'

Rafferty tried to inject a little humour. 'I thought you said not to mention that?' Unsurprisingly, it didn't go down too well.

'Don't get funny with me, you bastard.' By now, Jerry had totally lost the smooth estate-agent speak and reverted to his normal voice. It was thin with spite. 'I've a good mind to drop you in it.'

Alarmed, Rafferty soothed him. Luckily, he had remembered in time to call his cousin by his adopted name. 'Don't do that, Nigel. You might be the family's first estate agent, but surely you don't want to be its first grass, as well? Please. Trust me. I've sorted it.'

'You'd better have,' Jerry told him. 'I trusted you before and look where it's got me? I'm going upstairs to pack now while I wait for Terry's call. Your "sorting" had better have cleared me by the time I get home.'

Rafferty had thought it prudent not to mention to his cousin when he had rang him on Monday that his expensive designer suit would also have to be disposed of. Being too easily identified as the one Rafferty had borrowed, it would also have to form part of the 'burglar's' haul along with his passport and credit card. He sighed as the thought hit him again that it was something else for which he would be expected to pay. Unfortunately, after his self-administered pep talk, Rafferty had gone shopping on the Sunday after he had met Estelle and his purchases of new suits, shirts, etc, had put a serious dent in his credit card limit. He had invested in three new suits, six new shirts and another pair of Italian loafers. They were currently sitting in his wardrobe and taunted him every time he opened the door. So much for his 'investment'. God knew when he might next have an opportunity to wear them.

Uneasily, he wondered what Jerry would say – and do – when he discovered the ante had now been upped to *two* murders ... He didn't even dare to ponder how much it would cost him to buy his cousin's silence a second time.

Rafferty was beginning to think fondly of

his trouble free days as a sad, lonely, unloved git. He was still all those things of course, but now he had other worries. Joining the dating agency had brought more than its share of grief; so much for positive thinking, look where it had landed *him*.

But as he thought of Jenny and Estelle and their poor, slashed and battered bodies, he reminded himself that he still had his life. And where there was life there was hope. He must remember to tell that to Jerry.

It was later that week when Rafferty learned the one piece of good news to come his way since Bill Beard had broken his happiness bubble. And it came courtesy of Superintendent Bradley of all people. Although Rafferty felt sorry for Harry Simpson, he was relieved to learn that the fates should have played into his hands so swiftly.

'So, with Harry Simpson gone off on long-term sick leave, the Lonely Hearts case is now your baby.' Brusque as only a true Yorkshireman can be, Bradley dumped a pile of files about the murders on Rafferty's desk. 'Familiarise yourself. Go and see Simpson and pick his brains, see what he's been keeping to himself. When's Llewellyn back from honeymoon?'

'Monday.'

'You can have him on the team.' Bradley gave what for him passed for a smile. 'Posh lot at that dating agency,' he commented. 'All double-barrels and how-now-brown-cow accents, likely. You'll need Llewellyn's dainty touch. Not to mention his intellect.' Bradley added the acid reminder. 'It *was* your sergeant who solved your last case, wasn't it, Rafferty?'

Rafferty sat silent and grim-faced at Bradley's taunt, knowing he daren't defend himself. If he got his dander up, who knew what he might let slip? He consoled himself with the thought that, although he hadn't gone to university like Llewellyn, and whatever Bradley might infer, he wasn't about to be voted in as the village idiot.

But perhaps he was, he reflected, as Bradley slammed out of his office. After all, finding himself in charge of a double murder investigation in which he, or rather, his alter ego, Nigel Blythe, featured as chief suspect, wasn't the brightest of achievements.

How simple it had seemed at the time. His plans had slipped into place with a magical ease previously unknown to him. But of course the magic had turned out to be of the black variety which had used a siren's voice to lure him in. Now he was snared, good and proper.

But at least, he assured himself as he looked down at the pile of reports the super had dumped on his desk, by having this case under his own control he would be in a position to steer it away from his cousin. And while he waded through the pile of reports to 'familiarise' himself with the enquiry, he had the perfect excuse to avoid interviewing any of the other suspects. Better yet, Llewellyn would be back on Monday. Somehow he'd manage to palm most of the interviews off on to him. At least, by then, the changes in his appearance he had decided were necessary would have matured sufficiently to render the witnesses' recognition of him as Nigel Blythe far less likely. He hoped so, anyway.

Rafferty, now officially in charge of the case, made the time to get himself over to Harry Simpson's home. As the super had remarked, Harry Simpson had a habit of keeping certain things to himself in his investigations. Rafferty was desperate to find out if Harry had kept something back on the Lonely Hearts case.

Harry lived in a tiny flat in a shabby house on St Mark's Road, near the busy commuter station. The street was noisy, not only with the sound of trains, but also with through traffic and the revving of engines as people queued to get into the station car park a few yards down from Harry's front door.

As Rafferty parked and got out of his car, he reminded himself to stay in his own character and out of Jerry's. Harry Simpson might be sick unto death, but he was still sharp enough to notice if he let slip something that only Nigel Blythe could possibly know.

Rafferty pressed the buzzer for Harry's flat and waited. It was some time before Harry answered and released the front door. Rafferty climbed the stairs to the first floor, knocked and walked in through the door of the flat which Harry had opened for him.

Harry lived alone. Divorced by a wife tired of being a police 'widow', he was father to four children he barely knew and never saw. Now, stripped of family, home and money, the career for which he had sacrificed everything had also abandoned him.

The flat had two rooms plus a tiny kitchenette with bathroom off. It was a grim little place, the wallpaper faded circa 1950s drab and curling off the wall in places. The furniture screamed 'job lot of other people's discards'. But Harry had never cared about such things. Until he had finally gone on sick leave, home, whether the marital one or this dreary bachelor flatlet, had been a place he had spent little time. He rarely even ate there as the station canteen was both Harry's larder and cafe. The police force had been his life; even when not on duty or eating, he had still spent a lot of his time loitering in the station canteen to pick up snippets of gossip about other cases.

The only possessions of any interest in the living room were the mementoes of a lifetime in the police force. Scrapbooks of newspaper cuttings of his cases – both successes and failures – were piled high on every flat surface. Half-a-dozen commendations were piled in another corner, though on the floor this time and more carelessly than the newspapers. But then Harry Simpson had never thought much of his so-called superiors or their commendations. Invariably, as he had confided to Rafferty, they had been given at the wrong time and for the wrong reasons.

The gas fire was full on and churning out such a blast of heat that as soon as Rafferty entered the living room he began to sweat. Harry, though, looked to have no sweat in him. Bone-dry and brittle-looking, he appeared skeletal. The effort of answering the intercom in response to Rafferty's ring had clearly exhausted him. He lay collapsed in an old armchair that sagged nearly as much as Harry, breathing from an oxygen bottle.

Strange, thought Rafferty, that during all the weeks Harry had gritted his teeth and dragged himself into work, he had managed to stave off the exhaustion. It was clear he could stave it off no longer. The acceptance that he was unfit for work had finally allowed him to give in to his body's weariness; his body had taken advantage of such weakness to get its own back.

When he could get his breath, Harry gasped out, 'I know. I look like death. Just don't say it.'

Even Rafferty wasn't that tactless. He offered to make tea, his ma's cure-all, but Harry, long past such cures, shook his head. 'Can't stomach it. Make some for yourself. There's no milk.'

More to give him time to compose some non-incriminating questions about the case and for Harry to get his remaining breath back, Rafferty walked the few steps through to the tiny kitchenette, filled the electric kettle, plugged it in and began to assemble the makings of tea.

After a while, Harry asked, 'You said on the phone you've been assigned to the Lonely Hearts case.'

Rafferty came to the doorway and nodded.

'Thought you would be.' He sighed, adding, as if Rafferty was entitled to an explanation for his presumed lack of grit, 'I knew, when the second girl was found and I realised we might well be in for the long haul of catching a serial killer, that I wasn't up to it.' He gave a wry smile. 'You should have heard the super when I told him I wanted to be taken off the case. You'd think I got this bloody disease deliberately just to spite him.'

Rafferty could imagine. 'So you won't be expecting him to come sick visiting bearing a bunch of grapes and a bottle of Lucozade?'

'Every cloud has a silver lining.' Typically, Harry didn't waste time on self-pity. 'You've read the files?'

'Made a start, anyway,' Rafferty admitted cautiously.

Harry grinned. 'You and paperwork were never soulmates, were you? Suppose you want to pick my brains?'

'That's the general idea. Bradley seemed to think you might have kept something back from the reports.'

'Into casting aspersion as well now, is he?'

'And – have you?' Rafferty forced himself to ask.

He might as well not have bothered because Harry just said, 'All in good time,' and posed a question of his own. 'The first victim – the presumed Jenny Warburton – the one found behind the rubbish bins at the Cranstons' home – you managed to get a confirmed ID yet?'

Rafferty nodded. 'After you established that red hatchback left at the side of the Cranstons' house was hers it was always going to be unlikely that the body wasn't also. You said in your report that the Made In Heaven staff you'd managed to question denied that any Ms Warburton was at the party, which is a bit suspicious, as I know—' Abruptly, Rafferty broke off. He had been about to add that he knew that Jenny *had* been at the party as not only had Guy

Cranston introduced them, Rafferty himself had chatted to her for a sizeable part of the evening. His name – or rather, *Nigel's* – had been marked off on Caroline Durward's clipboard; surely Jenny's had been also? Of course, his had been marked off while he had been at the bar collecting refills, but hidden in the alcove as she had been for much of the early part of the evening, it was possible Jenny had been missed out, which would explain the discrepancy. From the reports Rafferty had so far waded through, it was clear that Guy Cranston had yet to be questioned about her presence.

'You were saying,' Harry prompted.

'What?'

'*As I know*, you said. *What* do you know?'

Harry's sunken eyes looked, to Rafferty's guilty conscience, to have a certain sly knowingness. He had the uneasy feeling that Harry was playing him like a gipsy violin. Quickly, he improvised. 'Just that the agency must have a record of her if she is one of their members.'

'According to Mrs Cranston – Caroline Durward as she seems to call herself – Jenny Warburton *is* a member. At least, she's on their computer as such. I hadn't been able to speak to Guy Cranston about the matter before I went sick. Although neither Mrs Cranston nor any of the other staff admit to knowing the girl, she seems to think a part-time member of staff took the Warburton girl on. They must have done, because she's certainly in the agency computer as being a member. Unfortunately, I was told this part-timer is currently on holiday and uncontactable.'

'Damn. That's inconvenient.'

'It's all in my records. I thought you said you'd read them? Missing Llewellyn, I take it?'

'I said I'd made a start,' Rafferty corrected. Harry's comment made him uneasily aware that his efforts to backtrack and appear to know nothing were as likely to place him under suspicion as knowing too much. It was going to be a very rickety bridge for him to balance on in the coming days. Scared now to open his mouth at all, Rafferty thought it wiser to say nothing.

Harry, after another penetrating stare, told him, 'The agency's rechecking their files. Said they'd get back to me. You'd better let them know you've taken over the case.'

Rafferty knew what he had to do, but he let Harry have his say and merely nodded, made his tea and sat down opposite his old colleague.

Harry stared at him as if only now taking in his changed appearance. It seemed to amuse him, if the harsh splutter that issued from his lips could be called laughter. 'So I was right,' he managed to force through the spluttering before a bout of coughing took over.

Rafferty licked suddenly dry lips. And though his mouth now felt as arid as Harry's laughter, the raised teacup made it no further, but hovered in mid-air while the scalding black tea slopped dangerously. 'Right about what?' he asked warily when Harry's coughing bout had subsided to a dull wheeze.

'About you being the man who we thought had done a bunk – the chief suspect, Nigel Blythe.'

Five

As Harry uttered Nigel's name, the hot tea jerked from Rafferty's cup and scalded his hand. He cursed, leapt from his seat and hurried through to the kitchen to run cold water over it. As the water gushed over his puckering flesh, he muttered to himself, 'How did he guess? How did I give myself away? What did I miss?'

But the damage was done. And little as he relished the prospect of Harry grilling him, he could hardly remain in the kitchen posing questions when Harry was the only one who knew the answers.

When he had sat down again, Harry held out a piece of paper. Rafferty looked at it for several seconds before he took it, as gingerly as if he feared it might suddenly grow a mouth and bite him. And as he looked at the paper, he suddenly found himself having to fight for breath as hard as Harry. For it was an artist's impression of his pre-disguise self and an excellent likeness.

'That's this so-called Nigel Blythe,' Harry told him. 'I take it you recognise him?'

Stunned, Rafferty could only nod. His hastily constructed cover-up had been for nothing, he realised. He might have known it would be a waste of time. Didn't murderers always give themselves away? But I'm *not* a murderer, Rafferty silently protested. Maybe not, but things were looking black for him. After he had told so many lies who was going to believe him now if he tried to protest his innocence? What would Superintendent Bradley say? Worse, what would he *do*? But Rafferty feared that was one question to which he *did* know the answer.

Shock had slowed his thought processes and it took him several more seconds to wonder why Harry had so far failed to report his discovery. He tuned back in to what Harry was saying to find out.

'Luckily for you, none of the witnesses could agree about Nigel Blythe's appearance. The witness who gave that description,' he nodded at the paper fluttering like a wounded butterfly in Rafferty's hand, 'came the closest, but I managed to wear him down until he doubted himself and ended up describing someone far less like you.' Harry's sunken eyes were again staring at Rafferty. 'Tell me I was right to do that.'

Rafferty managed to gasp out, 'You were right, Harry. Never doubt it.'

Harry simply nodded and handed him something else. 'You'll be wanting to lose this as well.'

'This' was a small cassette tape of the type used in telephone answering machines. 'It's from the Warburton girl's ansafone.'

Rafferty had been worrying about the messages he had left on Jenny's machine; Harry was offering Rafferty the lifeline *he* had been denied. Overcome with gratitude, Rafferty felt a desire to unburden himself. 'Let me explain—'

But Harry cut him off. 'Don't bother. I can't spare the energy required to hear how you managed to get yourself into this ridiculous situation. Just be glad I believe you didn't kill those girls.' As an afterthought, he added, 'And be even gladder that I feel reluctant to make our revered superintendent's week by supplying the evidence that would enable him to get both of us out of his hair.' He jerked his head at the tape. 'That's the only copy. Yours are the only messages on it. Take it away and destroy it.'

Rafferty nodded, began to thank him. But he wasn't sure whether Harry had heard him before the sick man's eyes closed and he dropped into an uneasy doze. Rafferty tiptoed to the door, the evidence clutched tightly to his chest, and let himself out.

After Llewellyn and Maureen's wedding, Rafferty, full of good cheer and Jameson's whisky, had persuaded them to meet up with him on their return from honeymoon. After all, as he had jovially reminded them, he had a vested interest in their marriage. Without him there might never have been a wedding.

Now, with so much on his mind, Rafferty wished he had kept his mouth shut. He wasn't feeling too sociable just now – in fact, he had turned into more of a shrinking violet than he had been for a large chunk of the dating agency's first party, scared every time he ventured beyond the station that he would attract the pointing finger and the accusation, 'But that's *him*. That's Nigel Blythe.'

But Llewellyn, punctilious about such tentative arrangements as he was about everything else, rang him on the Sunday morning to confirm it was still on. And Rafferty, aware it would look odd if he tried to get out of the arrangement he had proposed with such enthusiasm, had no choice but to agree.

He practised happy smiles in front of the mirror before he set off. Every one looked strained and unnatural. With a fatalistic shrug, he turned away. At least he would get Llewellyn's reaction to his new look now rather than when he returned to work the next day. The last thing he wanted was for the Welshman's comments to start his other colleagues off again with more uncomplimentary remarks about his new look and for someone to begin to wonder what had really prompted it. Fortunately, thanks to Harry Simpson, none of them had had the opportunity to see the police artist's best effort at capturing the face of the supposed 'Nigel Blythe'. Even more fortunately, the artist was new and had never met Rafferty. Rafferty did his best to keep it that way.

He and Llewellyn arranged to meet at The Black Swan. It was near to Rafferty's flat so he could walk there. Neither Llewellyn nor Maureen drank alcohol so they didn't mind driving. He wondered what they would have to say about his altered appearance.

He didn't have to wait long to find out. From behind his recently acquired spectacles, Rafferty squinted round the saloon bar. With difficulty, he located the tanned and happy pair at a corner table. He joined them, being extra careful to avoid tripping over the furniture on his approach.

He forced out a jaunty, 'How do?' by way of greeting. 'So how was the honeymoon?'

They both glanced up at him and did a double-take.

'New look,' he explained in as airy a fashion as he could manage as he sat down. They had got him a drink while they awaited his arrival and now Rafferty picked up the pint of Adnams bitter and swigged a third of it back. 'Was getting stuck in a rut,' he enlarged. 'So what do you think?'

Maureen was the first to recover. 'Did somebody turn your head upside-down?' she asked.

Rafferty managed a wry smile and waggled his spectacles at her. 'These are at the top end, so I'm definitely the right way up.'

Llewellyn took a contemplative sip of his orange juice before he ventured a comment. 'Glasses? They're new.'

'Mm. Been getting headaches. Optician said I was suffering from eye strain. Not getting any younger, I suppose.'

Llewellyn looked surprised. As well he might. He'd only been away for two weeks and Rafferty had never before mentioned headaches or eye strain.

'What can you possibly have been doing since we went on honeymoon to damage your eyesight so much you need spectacles?'

'Probably been trying to read his own handwriting,' Maureen tartly remarked.

'You *have* rather come to rely on my notes during an investigation,' Llewellyn commented. 'But even so—'

'Does it matter what caused it?' Rafferty demanded irritably. He repeated in a Bradley-brusque tone, 'As I said, I've been getting headaches.'

'You *do* drink rather a lot. In fact, I—'

'In fact – nothing. It's nothing to do with drink,' Rafferty insisted. 'I told you what the optician said.'

'Which one did you go to? Only I can recommend an excellent optician if you want a second opinion.'

Trust Llewellyn to be ready with advice. He didn't even wear glasses.

'He has a large range of attractive designer frames.' The stylish Llewellyn eyed Rafferty's horn-rimmed spectacle frames with a moue of distaste.

Rafferty couldn't altogether blame him. They were an old pair of his late father's that he'd helped himself to when he'd taken his ma home from their recent shopping-cum-burglary expedition. Considering how warped they made his vision it was a wonder he *didn't* have headaches. Judging by the style – or lack of it – the frames were first generation National Health Service. But time had been pressing and choice not an option. 'I like them,' he lied. 'I think they do something for me.'

'Yes, but what?' Maureen asked with saccharine sweetness. 'Were you trying for the intellectual look?' Her tone suggested he'd fallen short.

Llewellyn at least had no acerbic comment to make, beyond the plaintive, 'You don't look like yourself. It's disconcerting.'

Relieved to hear the first of Llewellyn's observations, Rafferty had to agree with the second. His appearance disconcerted Rafferty as well, each time he looked in the mirror. Stranger still, now, instead of shaving his face every day he had to keep going to the barber to keep the No. 1 in prime Premier style.

Although Rafferty had insisted after their wedding that since he and Llewellyn had become family Llewellyn should give over 'sirring' him, now he drew rank. 'My round, I think. Same again, Sergeant?' he pointedly asked as he picked up the glasses. 'Are we all having the roast beef? If so, I'll get it ordered before they run out.'

At least his drawing of rank had the desired effect. Because Llewellyn's brown eyes simply looked sharply at him, he nodded a yes to each of Rafferty's questions and said no more.

As he stood at the bar waiting to be served, Rafferty could see Llewellyn and Maureen reflected in the mirror behind the bar. They were whispering together and giggling. Llewellyn *giggling*? What next? Drinking pints of Adnams with whisky chasers? Rafferty scowled. Then he caught sight of himself in the mirror and was disconcerted all over again. Maureen's arch comment hadn't been entirely undeserved. Between his heavy horn-rimmed glasses, his new-grown and somewhat rusty-looking beard and his No. 1 haircut, he looked a cross between a mad polytechnic lecturer and a football hooligan.

His own mother had trouble recognising him. But at least, when he was finally forced to face them, his new look made it less likely that any of the dating agency's clients or staff would look at him and see Nigel Blythe. It was a comforting thought.

By the time he was finally served in the lunchtime crush and returned with fresh drinks, it became clear that Llewellyn and Maureen had concluded that their wisest course was to ignore his altered appearance. Because as soon as he sat down they began a determined description of what they had seen on their honeymoon tour of the sites of Ancient Greece, which continued as they ate their meal and didn't stop till an hour later when Rafferty, overdosed on ancient wonders, said he had to go.

'But you haven't told me anything about this latest case,' Llewellyn protested. 'The one the media is calling the Lonely Hearts murders. Don't—?'

'Time enough for that tomorrow, Dafyd,' Rafferty told him gruffly. 'You're just back from honeymoon, man. Can't you leave it till then before you start neglecting your new wife?'

Scared in case Llewellyn persisted and pushed him into revealing the name of the chief suspect, Rafferty made a swift exit before he got the chance. He was relieved to get out of the pub and not just to avoid discussing the case with Llewellyn after downing a few relaxing beers. It was his cousin Maureen's presence which was the inhibiting factor. Because Rafferty knew if he were to start discussing the case with Llewellyn and Nigel Blythe's name should slip out, Maureen would be on to it in a flash. Well, Nigel *was* her cousin, too. She would immediately reveal the Rafferty family connection. And anyone making a connection between himself and Nigel Blythe was the last thing he wanted.

He was thankful to reach the sanctuary of his flat without seeing anyone who knew him. Once safely inside, he yanked off his glasses and slumped down in an armchair. Thanks to the prescription lenses of his father's spectacles, his head was now throbbing in earnest and he swallowed a couple of aspirin to deaden the pain. He might, so far, have managed to avoid being questioned about the murders, but he was still being punished for his deception in other ways. In his haste to adopt a disguise it had never occurred to him that his father's prescription lenses might be a disguise too far.

But it was too late now. He would have to continue to wear them until the case was solved. He only hoped he didn't end up half blind.

The next morning, Llewellyn was in the

police station bright and early. Rafferty found him hovering like an alert greyhound when he reached his office. And as he studied the witness's statements, Dr Sam Dally's post-mortem findings and the grisly photographs of the two dead girls, Llewellyn commented, 'Looks to me as if we might have a misogynist on our hands.'

'A whatonist?' Rafferty asked with a frown that blurred his already blurred vision even more. His headache was back with a vengeance. It made concentration difficult.

'A woman-hater. A man with a pathological loathing of women. According to Harry Simpson's reports and Dr Dally's post-mortem findings, both victims were killed in a frenzied blood-letting. There was *hatred* there. Although it seems likely they died quickly, both women must have experienced some moments of pure terror.' Llewellyn paused before he added bleakly, 'And now another young woman seems to have gone missing.'

Rafferty's head jerked up. The pain was but a moment behind and he winced when it caught up. 'What did you say?'

Llewellyn waved one of the reports at him. 'Have you not yet seen this?'

'No.' Rafferty leaned forward in his chair and snatched the paper from the startled Llewellyn. Too hasty, he told himself. His eyes flew over the report, but he couldn't focus on it. Impatiently, he snatched the glasses from his nose and while he pretended to clean them he hurriedly read through the latest report, appalled to learn that Isobel Goddard hadn't turned up for work. Nor was she at her flat. Dear God, he pleaded, not another one.

Don't panic, he warned himself. Then he remembered Lancelot Bliss had said her parents owned a decaying pile somewhere in Suffolk. 'Maybe she's gone home to her family? It's what I'd do, if I were Isobel Goddard, after the murder of two young women so close to home. Give the agency a ring, Dafyd. They should have a number for her next-of-kin.'

Rafferty let out a silent, relieved sigh when after a couple of phone calls Llewellyn established that Isobel was safe and well in Suffolk. But his relief was short-lived, as next Llewellyn turned his attention to Rafferty's cousin.

'This Nigel Blythe,' he began.

Rafferty looked up and asked warily, 'What about him?'

'According to the files, he seems to have disappeared. He's not at home. At least, he's not at the address he gave the agency, though as there seems to have been a delay in checking there he must have had ample time to make his escape.'

Rafferty, who had failed to update the

reports, sat back and told him, 'Actually, Mr Blythe's back now.' He didn't need to add that he was still chasing the paperwork as Llewellyn knew him of old. 'He was away from home for a while, in York, or so I understand.' Rafferty forced himself to act naturally, and to ask, 'But do you think it's suspicious that Blythe was absent from home at the very time he's suspected of involvement in the deaths of two young women?'

Llewellyn gave the tiniest shrug. 'It's just that April's an odd time of year to holiday in England, if that's the reason he was in York.'

'You've just come back from an April holiday yourself.'

'Honeymoon,' Llewellyn corrected. 'Hardly the same thing, especially since we went to Greece, our decision to get married was sudden and we had to take the date the Registrar could give us.'

Their decision to get married had been all too sudden from Rafferty's point of view. He would, he suspected, never forget the panic the news had brought. 'Anyway, April's perhaps not such a strange month to holiday if you're an estate agent, like this Nigel Blythe. I presume they have to take their holidays in the quiet times, before the house buying and selling market hots up. Besides, he wasn't on holiday. I spoke to him on the phone.' He had, too, officially. He had felt he had to try to follow his normal routine during the investigation. To do otherwise would look odd. He'd got another ear-bashing for his pains when he'd broken the news that Nigel was now in the frame for two murders, not one. 'He said he was at some estate agents' jamboree.'

Rafferty could feel Llewellyn studying him and wondered what he'd said to give himself away *this* time. Feverishly, he checked over what he'd said and was relieved to discover he'd said nothing to give himself away as a Nigel impersonator. So why was Llewellyn staring at him as if he couldn't believe his eyes?

Rafferty ran his hand over his head and realised his hair needed its No. 1 scalping redone. And as he looked down and saw his father's spectacles sitting on his desk, he felt a moment of horror. He'd taken them off to clean them and in his shock about Isobel Goddard seemingly going missing, he'd forgotten to replace them. Now, without the glasses and with his hair growing again, had Llewellyn connected him with one of the less accurate photofits of 'Nigel' that hung on the white board in the Incident Room? For a few, fleeting, heart-stopping seconds, Rafferty held his breath.

Then Llewellyn, his mood strangely playful, remarked, apropos of nothing at all as far as Rafferty could see, 'The cure seems to have taken.'

It was Rafferty's turn to stare. 'Cure?' he asked. 'What cure? What are you talking about?'

Llewellyn's lips turned slightly upwards. Whatever it was, it was obviously a good joke by the Welshman's dry standards.

'Don't you remember? At my wedding, you swore on some holy water your mother brought to the Register Office to sprinkle over us after our nuptials, that you'd give up producing outlandish theories on all future investigations.' Llewellyn's thinly handsome face twitched into a smile. 'Your Catholicism must be less lapsed than you thought for such a holy water swearing to be honoured. I've never known you to be so lacking in ready theories. Normally, you'd have seized on a suspect such as this Nigel Blythe and come up with all sorts of wild theories. Especially as the man's an estate agent.'

Llewellyn had learned that estate agents were not Rafferty's favourite people. The one through whom he had bought his flat had played fast and loose with him, getting him to raise his offer price several times by telling him he had another prospect keen to buy. It was only after his purchase had gone through that Rafferty had discovered the estate agent's deceit. There had been no other prospect as the seller had gleefully informed him.

Rafferty, who had no recollection of any holy water swearing, managed a wry grin. But he had been so relieved everything had gone off smoothly that he had got out of his head at the reception. The ceremony and pretty well everything else was just a blur in his memory. Still, his forgotten vow served a useful purpose. How else could he explain his uncharacteristic behaviour?

He managed a bright, 'I can do solemn swearings, Dafyd. Bloody brought up on the things, wasn't I? What with baptism and weekly confessions, confirmation and that *Soldier of Christ* malarkey, solemn swearings are like mother's milk to a good little lapsed Catholic lad like me.'

Rafferty now decided that the best approach to the inevitable 'Nigel Blythe' questions from Llewellyn was the bold one. Taking the tentative, careful route had never been his style and Llewellyn had spotted it immediately. Just as well he had made such an uncharacteristic statement about ending wild theorising at the wedding reception. But Llewellyn knew him well enough not to expect such a vow to last.

After checking his memory to remind himself whether or not he had actually learned *officially* about the burglary, he mentioned it to Llewellyn.

'A burglary?' Llewellyn repeated. 'Staged by an obliging friend after the first murder, do you think?'

Rafferty was non-committal on this. But it really was sod's law, he thought. Here he was, doing his damnedest to forswear wild theorising in the absence of any proven facts to back his theories, only to have the normally irritatingly logical Llewellyn take up the slack. But then Nigel Blythe *had* featured strongly thus far and between Harry Simpson's ill-health and Rafferty's taking over and official familiarisation with the case, his alibis had yet to be checked.

'This burglary is certainly a convenient excuse for the even more conveniently absent Mr Blythe,' Llewellyn went on. 'When is this burglary supposed to have taken place?'

'Nobody knows. The neighbours could tell us nothing.' Thankfully. 'A Mr Tierney reported the break-in. Says he's some sort of cousin of this Nigel Blythe and that Blythe had asked him to keep an eye on his apartment while he was away. Tierney said Blythe had told him he was attending this estate agents' do in York and the hotel confirmed he arrived before the first victim, Jenny Warburton, must have died.'

Rafferty felt a fleeting pang of loss as he spoke Jenny's name. Why hadn't he escorted her to her car? he asked himself again. If he had, she would still be alive.

'This Mr Tierney told me he rang Blythe on his mobile to let him know about the burglary and that Blythe was on his way home. I've spoken to him since, of course, but I felt I needed to get on top of all the reports before I saw him. If it's true, as he claims, that his passport's been stolen, he's not likely to be going anywhere. But I wanted to wait till your return before questioning him in person.'

Llewellyn looked quietly pleased at this as if Rafferty had just paid him a fulsome compliment. Perhaps he had. 'The first thing we need to do is find out if Blythe's alibi holds water. If it does, we'd better forget the thought that the answers are going to fall into our laps. If he *is* telling the truth, this case is still wide open. I'd like you to conduct the interview with Blythe, Dafyd. I'll act the role of silent observer. Maybe, if he *is* involved in these killings, it'll rattle him.'

The rattling of Jerry/Nigel was not top of Rafferty's agenda. The last thing he wanted was to further upset the cousin who held his future in his greedy estate agent's paws, especially after his earlier threat to 'drop him in it'. But, scared of what he or his still indignant cousin might inadvertently let slip after finding he was now chief suspect in a double murder investigation, he daren't question him himself. What if he was to call him Jerry by mistake? Letting Llewellyn do the questioning was the safer option as it would also be likely to make cousin Jerry more wary and careful in his answers. Hopefully, the whole procedure would be quickly over. All Jerry had to do was supply the details of the women who he said would alibi him and he'd be home free.

Rafferty took a piece of paper from the file in front of him and handed it to Llewellyn. 'Give him a ring,' he said. 'Let him know we're coming.' Rafferty had, of course, already forewarned his cousin. 'It's not as if he can't be expecting us. And as Superintendent Bradley used to be so fond of telling us, politeness costs nothing.'

Six

Rafferty hadn't seen Jerry since before the Lonely Hearts nightmare began. His stomach curdled at the thought of seeing him now because his cousin's phone-rage over his predicament had been bad enough, but in his increasingly lurid dreams Jerry met him and Llewellyn with an exposé of spittle-flecked fury.

Rafferty handed the car keys to a surprised Llewellyn, got in the car and spent the journey trying to figure out what he could say should his nightmare become reality. But he still had no answer by the time they had reached Jerry's apartment building and been buzzed in. Even Jerry's failure to say anything as he opened the door to his apartment didn't soothe his anxieties because the hard, accusatory stare he directed at Rafferty spoke volumes and promised more.

But to his surprise, after Jerry had listened with a bored, patrician air that implied his current predicament was tedious beyond belief while Llewellyn made the introductions, his cousin simply turned on his heel and led them into his apartment before he spoke.

'Really, it's too ridiculous.' After inviting them to sit down, Jerry, being the new Nigel, remained standing so he could lean the arm of his expensive suit in elegant insouciance in front of what Rafferty knew to be an Italian marble fireplace. 'I can't begin to take it seriously.'

Rafferty was relieved to hear it. And as Jerry shot his black silk cuffs with their gold, monogrammed cuff links, he conceded that Nigel, Jerry Kelly as was, did bored patrician even better than Isobel Goddard did rich. To distract himself from the worry that Jerry – Nigel – he *must* make himself think of him as Nigel – would soon tire of his effete *aristo* game-playing and revert to type, he mused on what piece of aristocratic flummery Nigel would come up with next; his own heraldic device perhaps? Crossed builder's hods and a bar sinister would be the most appropriate for the Kelly family; with a noose over all in remembrance of their several shared ancestors who had taken the long drop.

After having worried himself into nervous exhaustion about their reception, Nigel's play-acting grated on Rafferty. He longed to prick his cousin's posing bubble, but he quickly thrust the temptation away. He needed to keep Nigel sweet. Besides, he should be grateful his cousin not only showed no sign of making good his threat, but that he had used his practised estate agent charm to such effect that two married women were prepared to put their reputations on the line to provide him with alibis in a double murder investigation.

Languidly, Nigel gave the names and addresses of the women he claimed could alibi him. 'I think I can say with confidence that these ladies will confirm what I said. You'll find that one or other of them is able to vouch for me over a period of hours on Friday and Saturday evenings, certainly from seven in the evening till around midnight.' As he laid slender fingers against his Clintonesque coiffure, careful not to disturb its sleek chestnut sweep, he added, 'Discretion will be called for as these ladies are both married.'

As was Nigel, since, to Rafferty's certain knowledge, his divorce had not yet come through, though Nigel didn't trouble to mention that.

With the alibis now officially supplied, some of the shoulder-shrugging confidence that emanated from Nigel transplanted itself to Rafferty. Freed from the worry that Nigel's alibis might be mere mirages and that his cousin really had no reason, other than spite, to drop him in it, Rafferty felt some of the tension drain away. And as he glanced over at his *faux*-aristocrat cousin and caught another glimpse of the equally *faux*-aristocratic cuff links, he felt a snigger coming on. Because, for Rafferty, who so often seemed to be the one who landed head first in the dung heap, it was rather satisfying that for once, Nigel should find himself in a similar position. Fortunately, he was able to turn the snigger into a coughing fit that had Llewellyn urgently searching out the kitchen for a glass of water. But even as Llewellyn followed Nigel's pointing finger, Rafferty's amusement died a natural death. Because Nigel's trouble was only temporary and was as nothing compared to his own. And once Llewellyn had disappeared from sight, Nigel, clearly not fooled by Rafferty's snigger-turned-cough, took the opportunity to remind him of the fact.

Dropping the air of languid ennui he had adopted on being cast in the role of murder suspect, Nigel reverted to type and hissed in a furious whisper, 'I don't know what you think you've got to snigger about. In spite of your best efforts, you're the one really in the frame for these murders and don't you forget it, cos I won't. I can prove where I was on both nights, which is more than can be said for you. And at least I can get myself laid without having to sign up with dating agencies under borrowed names and borrowed documents like some poor, desperate, lonely gits I could name.'

Rafferty found it a salutary reminder. His amusement was but a memory by the time Llewellyn returned. Rafferty tossed back the water before he told Nigel, 'I'll speak to these women, Mr Blythe, and make sure they can verify what you say about your whereabouts. I'll get back to you as soon as I can.'

Nigel, again lounging nonchalantly on the marble mantelpiece, waved a languid hand and murmured, 'Whatever.'

Scarcely able to believe he was still free of suspicion, Rafferty made for the door as the bored aristo, Jerry Kelly, left them to find their own way out.

Before he drove up to York to interview the providers of Nigel's alibis, Rafferty called the team together in the Incident Room. He looked round at the assembled faces: DC Jonathon Lilley, intelligent and studying hard for his sergeant's exams; PCs Lizzie Green, much the same age as the two dead girls and keen as Lilley to find their murderer, and Timothy Smales, still wet behind the ears but now a little older and wiser after getting a few more investigations under his belt, Hanks, DS Mary Carmody and the rest. All were anticipating an announcement that Nigel Blythe was well and truly in the frame and all they had to do was prove his guilt.

Careful to position himself far from the board bearing the witnesses' photofit descriptions of 'Nigel Blythe', Rafferty took a deep breath, crossed his fingers behind his back and said, 'It looks like we may not be in for an easy ride after all as Nigel Blythe claims he has alibis. If they check out, we'll need to find the look-alike who stole his identity. Certainly, the Mr Blythe Sergeant Llewellyn and I spoke to earlier seemed confident of his alibis, isn't that so, Sergeant?'

Llewellyn had been unusually quiet during the return journey. And when Rafferty discovered what had been occupying his mind he was not best pleased.

'A little bit *too* confident, perhaps,' Llewellyn now suggested. 'I wondered if these alibis might not have been prearranged.'

Rafferty had no wish to go down that particular road. But he felt obliged to speak up for his cousin and his alibis. 'I can't believe that any woman – certainly no one-night stand as these two would seem to be – would provide a false alibi for a man suspected of two brutal murders.'

Having successfully shot Llewellyn's theory out of the sky, Rafferty waited for the flurry of speculation and moans to die down. Normally, he would have shared the disappointment that the easy solution was replaced by the hard slog of routine; but this time Rafferty was just relieved that *he* hadn't yet turned into that solution. 'Accept it,' he told them. 'Think of the overtime.'

He ignored the muttered 'yeah, and all of the unpaid variety, if I know Bradley', which issued from several sets of lips. 'Too much has been taken for granted already in this case.' He sent up a silent plea for forgiveness to the sick Harry Simpson who had saved his everything, before he continued. 'I want every witness, particularly those who were at either party, questioned again.'

This brought more *sotto voce* grumbles. 'I know it's a lot of work, a lot of repetition, but it must be done. Before we nail the murderer or murderers we need to be confident that any potential suspect has been *rightly* eliminated and not just because someone got sloppy in the belief that the case was already in the bag.'

'Both murders happened in closed environments, sir,' Mary Carmody pointed out. 'The simplest option is to take DNA samples from everyone present.'

'True,' Rafferty agreed. 'I put the idea to Superintendent Bradley, but he wasn't keen.'

Even though the DNA route would probably be less expensive in the long run, 'Long Pockets' Bradley had rejected the idea out of hand. The Super shared Scrooge's financial outlook and was reluctant to spend money on things that efficient detective work should provide. 'Maybe he'll reconsider when we've managed to reduce the list of suspects. But to turn from the realms of fantasy to reality, Sergeant Llewellyn has allocated a list of witnesses for each team to re-interview. Timings are going to be vital. Any alibi not substantiated by more than one person must be discounted. It's been known for killers to work in tandem, covering for one another, so check and double check.'

As the team took the lists and began to head for the door, Rafferty shouted after them, 'I shall want the results on my desk first thing in the morning. Smales, you stay here. I've got another job for you.'

Typically, Llewellyn had reserved for Rafferty and himself the list featuring Caroline Durward, Isobel, Farnell, Bliss, Dryden and Gifford. He had sat across a desk from Caroline for the best part of half-an-hour and as the others had also had ample time to study him, they were the ones Rafferty most wanted to avoid – certainly until he had more beard growth and another No. 1 haircut.

As the team left the Incident Room Rafferty told Llewellyn, 'You'll have to re-jig your lists. I've got to go to York to interview Blythe's alibis. You'll be in charge while I'm away. I'll take Smales with me to take notes.'

Whilst Smales grinned broadly at this decision, Llewellyn's features expressed doubt of its wisdom. 'It'll be good experience for the lad,' Rafferty insisted before Llewellyn could comment. 'And then, I think I'd better go down to Suffolk to question Isobel Goddard. See if she had any other reason for taking to her heels. Maybe she saw something that made her take fright.'

Fortunately, unknown to Llewellyn, he had taken the precaution of ringing the agency and when Isobel had answered he had put the phone down without speaking. So he knew she had returned to work, though nobody else knew he knew. It meant he wouldn't encounter Isobel when he drove to her parents' Suffolk home. Maybe, if Isobel *had* seen something that prompted flight, she would have mentioned it to her family, even if, thus far, she had failed to confide in either Harry Simpson or Rafferty.

It was odd that she should have chosen to return to Elmhurst if she had knowledge that could be dangerous to someone. Of course, he was, as yet, only surmising this was the case. She might, as claimed, have returned to her parents' home out of fear that a maniac was on a random killing spree.

He would have preferred to question the girl himself, but as Isobel Goddard was one of those he dare not yet encounter, he had no choice but to delegate the interview.

When he had so much personally riding on the outcome of the investigation it was frustrating to have to take a back seat.

'After that, I'll want to see the dead girls' families, which will need a woman's touch. I'll take Mary Carmody with me for that.'

All that should give him excuse enough to avoid the main witnesses for another day or two. Still worried that Maureen might expose to Llewellyn the family connection to Nigel, Rafferty was anxious to impress on him the need for discretion. He told Smales to change out of his uniform and to wait for him in the car park. When the young officer had left, Rafferty turned to Llewellyn. He was unsure quite how to tackle the issue. Llewellyn could be prickly. But it had to be done. Should Llewellyn mention Nigel's full name to Maureen she would immediately say, *'Nigel Blythe? If you mean the Nigel Blythe whose original name was Jerry Kelly, then he's my cousin. Mine and Joseph's.'*

If Llewellyn learned of the relationship then the chances of someone making the connection between him and the Nigel at the dating agency parties would be far greater. Alarmed by the danger inherent in such a connection, Rafferty felt he had no choice but to remind his sergeant of the need for confidentiality. Expecting Llewellyn's facial landscape to take on the appearance of frozen tundra on which Arctic terns could happily nest, Rafferty was astonished, once he'd stumbled through his awkward reminder, when Llewellyn's expression remained pleasingly temperate and his only comment was mild.

'I hope I've always respected the confidential nature of the work we do. I'm not the type of officer who returns home after work and bandies suspects' names about over the antipasta. I thought you knew that.'

'Well yes, of course I do. It's just that with a new wife, pillow talk – that kind of thing,' Rafferty tailed off lamely.

'*Pillow talk*?' Llewellyn repeated. He sounded more amused than offended. 'You can rest assured, sir, I don't do "*pillow talk*" about work matters. Maureen and I have many shared interests, but murder isn't one of them.'

Rafferty was glad to hear it. He managed a muttered, 'That's all right, then,' before he hurried off to find Timothy Smales in the car park.

Rafferty's journey up to York with Smales was uneventful. It was fortunate that he'd been able to 'borrow' Smales from uniform. A more experienced officer would certainly question Rafferty's determination to speak to the women alone. But Smales, being still apprentice-green, could, without argument, be despatched on tea-seeking duties or some such. He hadn't even expressed astonishment when told he could drive, but had simply taken the car keys with alacrity, as if scared Rafferty might change his mind. But as Rafferty told himself as he eased into the passenger seat, even Smales's driving had to be safer than his spectacled efforts. And it was less likely to wrap the car round a lamp-post.

And when, some hours later, as they pulled up in the hotel forecourt of the modern concrete and glass architectural monstrosity that was the four-star House of York, the hotel where the two women had agreed to meet him – being understandably reluctant to have him come to their homes – Rafferty began to believe the fates had relented and would treat him kindly.

For once, this optimistic belief wasn't disappointed. But then he had decided to help it along a little. His assurance that Nigel was an innocent whose identity had been stolen encouraged both women to back up Nigel's alibis. He had downplayed deliberately, certain that if they learned otherwise both women would retract. But his reassurance gave them confidence that their husbands would never discover how faithless they were. It had been a masterstroke.

He had interviewed each woman separately. Kylie Smith, all bleached blonde curls and short, hot-pink skirt suit – for all his high pretensions, in his love-life Nigel had reverted to type – seemed unable to speak in anything other than the clichéd phrases of the born estate agent and when Rafferty had pressed her for firm answers, she had done her best to convince him that her and Nigel's little liaison had been completely innocent.

'Nigel and I did have a little drinkette, Inspector, after dinner on the Saturday night. And although I admit I went up with him to his splendidly proportioned bedroom and we were there 'till almost midnight, it was only to look at his laptop and see how his property agency has designed their website.'

'Come and look at my website' must be the modern version of inviting a girl to look at one's etchings, Rafferty reflected. He'd have expected Nigel to have a more original chat-up line. But whatever his cousin lacked in originality was more than made up for by his choice of one-night stands. And as Rafferty realised that, as with Kayleigh Jenkins, Nigel's other alibi supplier, the time-scale Kylie Smith mentioned made it impossible for Nigel to have returned to Elmhurst to commit murder, he sent up a silent thank you. Because as he pocketed the two hand-written statements, he knew that Nigel was officially off the suspect list.

Fearing that even the bashful Smales would by now have managed to attract the attention of one of the four-star hotel's supercilious waitresses, place the tea order and return to make the astonishing discovery that Nigel Blythe wasn't at the top of their suspect list at all, Rafferty hastily drew the second interview to a close. With effusive thanks for her time, he ushered Kylie Smith from the room and went in search of Smales.

The drive back from York was the leisurely one Rafferty insisted upon. Unfortunately, it was also one with something of an 'atmosphere' because even though he had again allowed Smales to drive, this had done little to mollify the young officer's pique at being excluded from the interviews; neither had Rafferty's terse instruction to be quiet as he needed to think. After that, Smales had retreated into a sulky silence. It worried Rafferty because not only had his now silent companion become worryingly inquisitive, he had also questioned Rafferty's handling of the interviews, even going so far as to point out that he should have been present at both.

He was right, of course. Shame he hadn't realised just how much Smales had come on in the last few months. It was unfortunate that Smales's nous hadn't developed sufficiently for him to realise that questioning a senior officer's conduct of a case was unlikely to win him brownie points.

The only pleasing aspect to their return journey from Rafferty's point of view was that it provided more time both for his beard to grow and for the witnesses's memories of 'Nigel' to fade.

Seven

Back at the station, Rafferty quickly dismissed Smales. Anxious to avoid Llewellyn and receive another third degree about Nigel's alibis, he broke all records in typing up the notes of the York interviews that concealed as much as they revealed, and was about to head back out when he saw Llewellyn's message.

The first item on this lengthy epistle told him another thing he'd rather no one knew he knew; namely, that Isobel Goddard had returned from her parents' home and could be interviewed without Rafferty having to drive to Suffolk.

Why was it, Rafferty wondered, that whenever Llewellyn tried to be helpful, he invariably upset his own cunningly laid plans? Clearly, Llewellyn expected him to turn up at the dating agency offices. As this didn't suit Rafferty at all, he scribbled a brief note to the end of Llewellyn's, to the effect that he would be unavailable as he was interested to learn what Isobel's parents could tell him about the reason for her flight.

By now, as a quick perusal of the rest of Llewellyn's note revealed, the team, with minimal hands-on input from him, had managed to whittle the suspect numbers down by half. Isobel Goddard was still numbered amongst them.

With the discovery that Isobel had not been able to supply a verified statement as to her exact whereabouts for the approximate times of the two murders, Rafferty felt more need than ever to try to find answers to questions he had about the girl. After what he had learned about her at the first dating agency party he doubted her reason for returning to her parents' home after the murders provided the complete answer or even the real one. He hoped her parents might be able to shed some light.

It was a pleasant drive up to Suffolk. The Goddards' home, Latimer Court, was north of Ipswich and as traffic was surprisingly light he made good time until he tried to find the house itself. Latimer Court wasn't on a main road and even though he had rung Charles Goddard and obtained directions these had turned out to be totally confusing. So it was early evening before he finally noticed the sign for the house. Obscured by a privet hedge badly in need of a trim, it was only when a timely breeze raised the obscuring foliage that the worn lettering 'Latimer

Court' was revealed and he realised he had already passed the place three times.

He turned the car left and edged gingerly up a drive cratered with potholes and lined with knee-high weeds. Lancelot Bliss had said the place needed a lot of money spent on it. But even as Rafferty drove nearer to the house and saw its rundown state, he recognised that Latimer Court had once been a beautiful place and could be again. Elizabethan, laid out in the traditional 'E' design, it had the tall chimneys that were a feature of that era. Built of red brick mellowed to harmonious shades of rose, broken up by the many large creeper-clad casement windows, it was a romantic-looking house – at least from a distance. Though as Rafferty got nearer, he noticed the peeling paint on the woodwork, the dullness of the glass in the windows and that the chimneys, far from being engagingly picturesque, were in reality dangerously unstable. He guessed from the stains on the walls that the place also had a problem with damp.

Whatever might be wrong with the rest of the house, the front door looked as sturdy as the day the carpenter had fitted it. Huge, it was of silvery-grey oak with a knocker half as big as Rafferty's head. The woman who answered its reverberating summons turned out to be Mrs Goddard, Isobel's mother.

Eve Goddard must have been lovely in her

youth. Tall and willowy, she retained the good bones of true beauty, though Rafferty suspected the beauty was on the outside only. It wasn't age that had scored lines from nose to mouth and made those little puckering lines above her top lip that, in her case, surely betokened discontent rather than age.

Her greeting was cool. She led him to a room at the back of the house that he assumed had once been the library and left him there while she went to find her husband.

The room was as shabby as the rest. A large bookcase took up most of the wall opposite the windows. Half the shelves contained nothing but dust-balls and dead flies and the other half housed a collection of dun-coloured books that looked as though no one had opened them for half a century or more. In the centre of the room, eight chairs upholstered in cracked burgundy leather were set around a long table, all laced together by cobwebs; Rafferty half expected Dickens' Miss Havisham to appear, still in her tattered bridal dress.

Even though it was a bright day and the library had four floor-to-ceiling windows, the room was dim. He saw that the windows all had a thick film of grime made up of rain splatters, pigeon droppings and time's unwashed detritus. And as he peered through this misty miasma he glimpsed a secret garden that time – and the gardener – had long since forgot. It was all matted shrubs and roses strangled by the heavy embrace of bindweed. Beneath it all, he could just pick out what he thought must be part of the original herb garden. It was as choked and uncared for as the rest. He turned as he heard a hesitant footfall behind him.

'Inspector ... em...? My wife said you were here.'

It was clear Charles Goddard had already forgotten his name, so Rafferty repeated it.

'How can I help you?'

Charles Goddard was surely no more than in his mid-fifties, but with his grey, rapidly balding hair, vague manner and scholarly stoop, he looked ten years older. In his dark green cardigan that was missing buttons and had holes in the elbows he appeared as uncared-for as his home. He peered uncertainly up at Rafferty through spectacles held together with sellotape.

Rafferty said, 'I wanted to speak to you about your daughter Isobel, sir.'

'My daughter's not here, Inspector.' Eve Goddard appeared behind her husband. 'She's returned to her flat in Elmhurst. I drove her there myself.'

Rafferty nodded. 'It was you and your husband I wanted to speak to. I wondered whether your daughter told you what had prompted her to return here?'

'I'd have thought the murders in Elmhurst would be prompt enough for any sensitive young woman, Inspector,' was Eve Goddard's sharp response.

Charles Goddard added, more gently, 'They upset her so much that she could barely bring herself to talk about them at all. Not to me, anyway. She was closeted with her mother for most of the time she was here. I hardly saw her.'

'I asked because your daughter was apparently convinced she had been the intended target both times. Do you have any idea why that was?'

Charles Goddard gaped at him. 'Isobel? Surely not? You must have misunderstood her, Serg– er, Inspector.'

It was clear to Rafferty her father was the last person Isobel would confide in. He turned to Mrs Goddard. 'Did your daughter confide in you?'

'Confide?'

Her voice was sharp, her manner verging on the hectoring. Rafferty began to understand why her husband should appear so beaten down and defeated.

'Isobel had nothing *to* confide. As I have already told you, it was natural for her to return home in the circumstances. My daughter's a sensitive girl and had managed to convince herself she was next on the list of some psychopath.'

Charles Goddard chimed in. 'I don't understand why she went back to Elmhurst if that's the case.'

Neither did Rafferty.

'I told her she could give up that position my wife found for her,' Goddard said. 'I don't like to think of my daughter being alone in Elmhurst when there's a dangerous maniac on the loose.' Goddard turned to his wife. 'It's worrying, too, my dear, to think he might have attacked *you* that same night.'

'You were in Elmhurst on the weekend of the murders?' Rafferty asked.

Eve Goddard's beautifully sculpted lips thinned. 'Yes, but really, I can't think why you should question me on *my* movements. If you must know, I had found a wonderful dress for Isobel. I stopped at her flat that Friday night – the night I gather the Warburton girl was killed – to drop it off. I wanted her to have it for the party. I then drove her to the Cranstons' house.'

Rafferty recalled the man-bait dress and was astonished at the discovery that her own mother had bought Isobel such a revealing costume.

'And you really had no cause to worry about me,' she assured her husband. 'I was in no danger. I didn't even get out of the car.'

In her statement Isobel had made no mention of her mother dropping her off. Presumably she hadn't thought such information relevant. Mrs Goddard had appeared annoyed when her husband had mentioned it. Rafferty wondered why. Was it simply because she objected to being questioned? Or did she actually have something to hide? Whether she had or not, she was clearly a forceful woman. If it were up to her, Rafferty believed, the family fortunes would soon be revived.

Although, when questioned, she denied turning up at the second party also, with her looks, Rafferty didn't think she would have found it too difficult to persuade one of The Elmhurst's doormen to let her in. Or she could simply have asked her daughter for an official invitation.

Charles Goddard's mind was still on safety issues. 'I can only hope Isobel comes to her senses and returns home.' He turned to his wife and remarked, 'I said to you at the time, if you remember, my dear, that I thought working in a dating agency was not quite the thing.'

'It gives Isobel an income, Charles.' Implicit in Eve Goddard's voice was the rider that this was more than her husband managed. She didn't trouble to hide the contempt, though Charles didn't appear to notice this any more than he seemed to notice that the beautiful girl he had married had turned into a deeply frustrated woman.

'Still, as I said, that will soon be a thing of

the past.' Goddard's previously dull eyes had developed an enthusiast's sparkle as he turned to Rafferty and said, 'I've got plans, you know. Great plans.' Even his stoop seemed less pronounced. 'Chap was telling me about this marvellous idea—'

'Not another one.' Eve Goddard's mouth thinned. 'How many more?'

Goddard appeared oblivious to his wife's interruption. 'He said he'd made a packet in six months. All I'd need for capital is £5,000. I could raise it if I sold part of the library.' He gazed vaguely round. 'Some valuable first editions here, I believe.'

If there were, they were also veritable Houdinis at concealment. Rafferty, who had spent some twenty minutes in the library while he waited for Charles Goddard to appear, guessed if there had been valuable first editions, Eve Goddard would have long since realised their worth. As far as he could see, this 'valuable' library consisted mostly of snore-worthy collections of old sermons, dusty tomes by authors with unrecognisable names, piles of torn paperbacks and several teetering yellow towers of *The Times*.

Goddard, clearly intent on making the most of his captive audience, explained the 'marvellous idea'. To Rafferty it sounded like a classic scam. He began to give Goddard his opinion, but Goddard waved his doubts away.

'I'm sure you mean well,' he said, 'but you're quite wrong, my dear chap. You're a policeman, don't you see? You haven't the entrepreneurial flair required to get such a scheme off the ground. You would need the contacts, too, of course.'

Goddard's voice petered out as he realised he'd implied that Rafferty couldn't possibly have the contacts required. But although his voice trailed away, the light of the born enthusiast still burned in his eyes. After seeing Eve Goddard's reaction to this latest wheeze and hearing the exasperation in her voice, Rafferty realised Goddard was the type of man who would always see yet another new Jerusalem on the horizon. Hadn't Lancelot Bliss and Ralph Dryden made some acerbic comment about this tendency? It seemed clear that no matter how many false dawns lighting the way he'd already seen, Goddard would still be marching purposefully towards Jerusalem when they took him away either to jail or a rest home for the serially deluded.

Rafferty – whose family had always been poor – had the novel experience of feeling sorry for a man who had once had everything life could offer, but who had thrown it all away chasing rainbow-gold. He began to understand something of Eve Goddard's frustration.

For how many years had Isobel witnessed

this same scene and her mother's contemptuous treatment of her father? When had it begun? She was 27 now and he recalled Lance Bliss saying she had been around 12 when her father had made his disastrous investment. So, from an impressionable age and through fifteen long years after, she had seen the man who should have been the most important male in her young life abused and derided. Was that what had made her view all men as empty vessels worthy only of exploitation?

Charles Goddard appeared ineffectual and unlikely to restore the family fortunes, but he was still able to delude himself that one or another hare-brained scheme would provide the answer to the family's money problems. Rafferty was surprised a realist like Eve Goddard had stayed around long enough to witness yet another grand plan unfold.

Though he questioned them further, it was clear Charles Goddard could tell him nothing more. As for Mrs Goddard, Rafferty thought it was probably more a case of *wouldn't* than couldn't. Even if she didn't strike Rafferty as the most caring mother in the world, she seemed determined to reveal nothing more than what she had already told him.

It was as Charles Goddard escorted him to the door that Rafferty's eye alighted on the woodworm-raddled oak staircase. It was lined with portraits; most, to judge by the costumes, of long-dead people.

Goddard noticed Rafferty studying this dark and dusty collection and told him proudly, 'My ancestors, Serg–Inspector. There have been Goddards living here since 1565, when my namesake, another Charles Goddard, built the house. He's that rather villainous-looking character at the bottom.'

Goddard pointed to the portrait of a swarthy-skinned individual at the lower turn of the staircase. Dressed in scarlet velvet and lace, he reminded Rafferty of Charles II, but without the charm.

'Bit of a Casanova where the ladies were concerned,' Goddard confided. 'Ruthless too, if the family stories that have been passed down are to be believed. The man couldn't stand rivals at any price. He had a particularly effective way of seeing them off by arranging to have them attacked by footpads and run through with a sword. Rumour had it that old Charles wielded the sword himself.'

'Handy to have your very own gang of cut-throats,' Rafferty observed. 'Must iron out life's little problems a treat.'

Goddard shrugged. 'I suppose so. But the rumours did for him in the end, especially when he ran through one of Queen Elizabeth's favourites. He ended up on the gallows.'

Rafferty shuddered. 'Direct ancestor of yours, is he?'

'Yes. He's my great, great ... What is it now?' Goddard looked bemusedly along the row of portraits as if he expected one of them to come up with the answer. 'Is it ten or eleven greats? I can never seem to get it right. Anyway, he's my however-many-greats grandfather. It's funny how every generation seems to produce someone in his mould.' Goddard attempted a little joke. 'Thank God they've done away with hanging.'

Amen to that, thought Rafferty as, a minute later, the massive front door closed behind him. But even as his neck was gratefully shrugging off the rough noose imagination had dropped around it, he couldn't help but wonder whether, concealed beneath the make-up, the designer clothing and the décolletage, Isobel might not be the current generation's chip off cut-throat Charlie Goddard's block.

He started up the engine and bounced back up the drive to the road. How had she felt when the burden of saving the family had been thrust on to her shoulders? Desperate and frustrated, like her mother? Or determined, like her father's namesake? And if delusion was another family inheritance, like ruthlessness in ridding oneself of love rivals, was it possible that Isobel had thought if she removed Caroline then Guy would marry her?

Of course, the difficulty there was that it hadn't been Caroline Cranston who had been murdered. But if he was putting Isobel in the frame there was an answer to that little difficulty. Not only was Isobel extremely short-sighted, she was also very vain and refused to wear spectacles. And – as he had overheard at the first agency party – since she had tried and failed to get used to contact lenses, she was reduced to a half-world of vaguely formed faces and red rhododendrons that closer inspection turned into tractors. No doubt, even now, she was saving madly for one of those laser treatments that would remedy the problem.

The fact that she was more than half-blind wouldn't have assisted her in correctly identifying her victim. Both murder scenes – the Cranstons' car park and the grounds of The Elmhurst's annexe – had been dimly lit. Easy enough to mistake identities when the two victims had been dressed in similar clothes to Caroline Cranston and shared a superficial likeness to her.

Of course, the fact that both murder scenes had been poorly lit meant that others, too, would have found it difficult to correctly identify the chosen victim. Maybe, if Isobel had a guilty secret that gave her a valid reason for suspecting she had been the intended victim both times, she had been right to flee for her life.

It had been a long day. Rafferty was tired by the time he got back to the station. He had anticipated some peace and quiet while he studied the latest reports and had to bite back the irritation when he saw Llewellyn hovering by his office. He had hoped to avoid Llewellyn's questions for a while longer, but as that hope vanished he led the way into his office.

'I was just about to make a start on the reports,' he told Llewellyn as they both sat down and before Llewellyn had a chance to question him about his trips to York and Suffolk. 'But seeing as you're here you might as well tell me if you've found out anything new.'

'Depends what you call new. A number of other witnesses have also now stated that there was something odd about this Nigel Blythe.'

'The *supposed* Nigel Blythe, you mean.' Keeping it as brief as possible, Rafferty told him that the real Nigel Blythe's alibis had both held up. 'What do you mean by "odd", anyway?' he asked.

'The agency clients I've spoken to all said they thought he seemed to be pretending to be something he wasn't. From your discoveries in York it would appear they were correct. For one thing, he wore an extremely expensive suit but it didn't fit him properly.'

'Presumably, if he's the man who burgled the real Nigel Blythe's flat, he helped himself to the suit at the same time as he took Blythe's personal documents. Mr Blythe told me when I spoke to him on the phone that he was missing an expensive designer suit from his wardrobe.'

Llewellyn nodded. 'And then there was his accent. It kept changing, apparently. Not that he said much; not to the men anyway. One witness, a Mr Ralph Dryden, actually called the man *furtive*. He said he seemed reluctant to reveal anything about himself, though several of the other witnesses I spoke to were of the opinion that he seemed keen to get the two victims on their own. They told me he seemed to have plenty to say to them.'

'Mm. What do you make of it?'

'If it wasn't for the facts of the two murders I would have thought him simply someone intent on a bit of social climbing, hoping to find a woman of means to support him. Most of the members of that agency, male and female, hold down high-powered careers with commensurate salaries; highly attractive to the kind of man intent on battening on some lonely woman for an easy life.'

Not the most flattering description of himself Rafferty had ever heard. He forced out another question, 'And *with* the facts of the murders?'

'I think we must assume he burgled Nigel Blythe's apartment with the intention of setting himself up with an identity that would enable him to meet and murder women of the professional classes. We must assume that means premeditation; premeditation from a determined and extremely dangerous psychopath. We know from the security arrangements at both venues that – unless we're dealing with a deranged partnership of an agency member with an outsider, as you earlier suggested was a possibility – it's unlikely any outsider could have gained access. It leaves us no alternative if we're to launch a manhunt but to check out the tiniest fact about this man. And as he seems to have deliberately targeted Nigel Blythe in his identity theft, Mr Blythe merits further questioning. It seems likely the murderer must have known him in some capacity – maybe he bought a house from Mr Blythe's estate agency? But of one thing I'm certain – there's a connection of some sort. There has to be.'

Rafferty forced down the bile that had risen from his stomach. This was the conclusion he had most feared Llewellyn would reach. Because if they investigated each of his cousin's known contacts, how could they possibly miss *him*, or the fact that he had inexplicably failed to mention the relationship at all?

Eight

Thankfully, by the time Llewellyn returned to the station it was too late in the evening for him to begin checking out Nigel's contacts. At home, Rafferty spent the intervening hours considering what time-consuming task he could give Llewellyn that would leave him unable to make a start on the check. The answer came to him as he mentally reviewed the statements the team had collected during the day. Guy Cranston had said a cabbie had rung through on the intercom some ten minutes after he had seen Nigel leaving the first party with Jenny Warburton, to get him to open the gate. As the supposed Blythe was the only person Cranston recalled leaving around that time, he had presumed Blythe had ordered the cab.

Rafferty seized on this information with relief. Checking round the local cab firms would keep Llewellyn's sharp mind engaged in a harmless pursuit that would have no chance of leading back to Rafferty's 'Nigel'.

The next morning, Rafferty paid a flying

visit to the station. He read the latest reports, instructed the team on the tasks he expected them to complete and then, before Llewellyn or anyone else could complain or remind him of the need to check out Nigel Blythe's friends, family and acquaintances, he took off with Mary Carmody for the interviews with Jenny and Estelle's friends and families.

Rafferty decided he would speak first to Jenny's flat-mate. The flat they had shared was conveniently situated above a corner tobacconist in Elmhurst's High Street. Being on the corner, it had a double aspect on to the High Street and Penance Way and was both bright and spacious. The furniture was mostly modern, but there was an attractive old roll-top desk and several other older pieces. And as Rafferty guessed from what he had learned about her that these must have been Jenny's choice, he felt the loss of her all over again.

Grace Thurlow, Jenny Warburton's flat-mate, was a plain girl with a beaky nose and limp, sandy hair that was in need of a wash. Dressed in faded Indian cotton that was as limp as her hair, she seemed an unlikely flat-mate for the beautiful Jenny. Grace's thin lips were down-turned and Rafferty thought it likely the girl's natural expression was a sullen one, but for some reason she exhibited an almost Uriah Heep-like eagerness to please which brought some much-needed colour to her face. At first this puzzled him. But then it struck him that the ungracious Grace, with her oh-so-helpful air, was trying, insidiously, to paint a picture of her late flat-mate as being a young woman of few morals. One who was 'always out', and 'had lots of different men ringing her up and buying her expensive presents'.

Jenny hadn't struck Rafferty that way, far from it. He suspected Grace Thurlow had been jealous of pretty Jenny, Jenny with the neat nose, creamy skin and glorious fall of blonde hair, whom men had undoubtedly found far more attractive than they would the Grace Thurlows of this world. The girl would have annoyed him more had it not been for his recognition that, like him, Grace Thurlow was alone and lonely and likely to remain so unless she adopted a more positive attitude to life's difficulties. Though when he recalled where adopting a positive attitude had landed *him*, he wasn't sure he could recommend it.

'That was why I was surprised when you said she had joined this dating agency,' Grace told them. 'As I said, she wasn't short of men friends. But then Jenny could be very secretive.'

Sly, was the undoubted implication inferred. Rafferty hadn't noticed any slyness about Jenny either.

'Maybe she was dating a married man,' Mary Carmody suggested.

Grace shook her head. 'That couldn't be it. Though Jenny dated a lot, she always steered clear of them.'

Rafferty was surprised that Grace should be honest enough to admit that the immoral Jenny she had painted had some standards. He wondered again how two such dissimilar young women should have become flat-mates and he questioned her about it.

'Jenny's previous flat-mate went off to Australia with a boyfriend for a gap year between leaving university and getting settled in a career,' Grace explained. 'And Jenny hadn't got around to organising a replacement. This flat's expensive, so I think she must have begun to find it difficult to pay all the rent herself, so when a mutual acquaintance introduced us and Jenny learned I was looking for a place to live, she asked me to move in. That was six months ago.'

'Can you think of anything in Jenny's life that could make her the target for a murderer?'

Grace shook her head.

'Did Jenny never mention whether she'd met someone recently, someone who might be stalking her, say?' He knew he was clutching at shadows, but until he could find the real reason – insane serial killers aside – for Jenny's and Estelle's murders, shadows and shadowy theories were all he had.

And although Grace shook her head, he felt a dart of pure adrenalin when she frowned and added, 'Though, now I think of it, I wonder if she *had* met someone special because she became rather moony-eyed during the last few weeks before she died and would sit just staring into space with a smile on her face. I asked her if she'd met Mr Right, but she didn't answer me.'

Harry Simpson had already ascertained that Jenny hadn't confided her secrets to a diary. So who *had* she shared them with? 'Did Jenny have any close girlfriends? Someone with whom she might exchange secrets?'

'I told you, Jenny tended to be secretive, not much given to confiding. She told me she hadn't been close to her family since her parents' divorce five years ago. If she told anyone her secrets, it would be her previous flat-mate.'

Rafferty obtained the Australian phone number of Alison Curtis, Jenny's ex-flat-mate, from Grace before they left. Harry Simpson had already searched Jenny's bedroom and desk for any clues to her murder, but he had found nothing. Rafferty managed to contact Alison Curtis later that day after trying fruitlessly all morning; no doubt, student-like, she had been out enjoying Sydney's night-life. But while her desire to help was sincere, apart from confirming

Grace's belief that Jenny had been seeing someone special she was able to tell them little more and could supply no details.

Like Grace Thurlow, Rafferty found it puzzling that Jenny should have joined a dating agency if she *had* already found a 'special' man. He could only suppose he hadn't turned out to be so special after all. Poor Jenny, he thought. But whether or not the relationship had still been ongoing at the time of her death, Rafferty needed to discover the man's identity. And as he and Mary Carmody continued on their busy interview round, he wondered how to achieve this. The man hadn't come forward. He was probably keeping his head down just as Rafferty was; not because he was necessarily guilty of anything, but because he had no desire to get caught up in a murder enquiry. Such natural reticence had Rafferty's sympathy. It was a shame it frequently made the job more difficult.

It was late by the time Rafferty and Mary Carmody got back to the station. Llewellyn still hadn't returned. Checking out all the local taxi firms had been a longer job than he'd dared hope. But while Rafferty was happy to keep Llewellyn busy on routine enquiries so as to delay his question and answer session with Nigel, he wasn't pleased that his own day had proved fruitless. For all the hours they had put in with the dead girls' friends and families they had learned little of value. It made Rafferty rather heartsick to think they were getting no further forward in finding the real killer. How much longer could he go on telling lie after lie to protect his cousin and himself?

Two young women had been brutally slain. Was he being totally selfish, callous even, in concentrating much of his energy in getting himself and his cousin out of their predicament?

He carefully considered the question. But in spite of his feelings of guilt, in spite of all the lies, Rafferty didn't think his behaviour unwarranted. He had only to remember Jenny and Estelle as they had been to know his motives were fuelled more by the desire to avenge their deaths. He wanted their killer to face justice, but to have any hope of achieving this end he needed to remain free and untainted by suspicion. Still, Rafferty reminded himself, he couldn't be doing too badly. He *was* still free, still running the investigation. Admittedly that owed more to Harry Simpson's belief in his innocence than his own guile. It was strange that Harry should choose to give him the benefit of the doubt, for, although they'd worked amicably enough as colleagues for years, they'd never become really close. Harry had always been what Rafferty secretly feared he would become himself – a lonely man married to the job.

When the footsore Llewellyn returned to the station he revealed what Rafferty already knew, but which, thankfully, Llewellyn had taken most of the day to discover: Cranston's supposition about the taxi driver being 'Nigel Blythe's' was correct.

'A man calling himself Nigel Blythe rang Elmhurst Taxis to pick him up from The Huntsman in town around seven on the Friday evening, and take him to the Cranstons' house.' Llewellyn subsided in a chair looking so exhausted that Rafferty felt even more guilt-filled. 'The same driver confirmed he also collected this man from the Cranstons' at ten that same evening and dropped him in the centre of Elmhurst. His description tallies with those the party guests supplied.'

Rafferty nodded. He'd needed a drink, he remembered. One that wasn't wine, both to calm himself down and to celebrate meeting Jenny...

'I asked the cab driver if his passenger had any bloodstains on his clothing; he said not, which indicates he must have brought some protective covering with him, which again confirms these murders were premeditated. But even now we've traced the cab driver, it doesn't get us much further forward. We still know so little about this character. All we *are* sure of is that whoever he is he's not the real Nigel Blythe.'

Llewellyn continued. 'The Huntsman is obviously not a regular haunt of this imposter. He probably picked a public house he had never previously used in order to help conceal his identity. Certainly, none of the staff recognised him from the photofit, though one said he thought he recalled the man used the public phone to ring for the cab. And since that line has brought us to a dead end I think it's time to question Nigel Blythe again. I'm sure, if he's carefully questioned, there must be *something* he can tell us.'

Rafferty was sure of it, too.

'I'd like to call and see him tomorrow, first thing.'

Rafferty knew it would be unwise to put Llewellyn off again. But as soon as Llewellyn had left for home, Rafferty rang his cousin on his mobile and – for yet another consideration – plea-bargained his continued silence.

With both his emotions and his wallet worn out, Rafferty wished he'd conquered his technophobia and gone the internet dating route. But for all the computer courses the super had forced him to attend, he was still a reluctant geek. And as for the personal ads in the local papers, his perusal of the first half-dozen with their extravagant claims had put him off looking further. So, obstinately, he had clung to the belief that a professional agency, one that was a member of a professional body, the ABIA – The Association of British Introduction Agencies, which had been 'setting standards for the UK's introduction services since 1985' – would, for him, be the best route. They offered discretion and would not waste his time – or his anticipated repeat membership fee – by raising unwarranted hopes about a fellow member's personal attributes.

And so it might have proved if the Made In Heaven agency hadn't been targeted by a murderer.

When he arrived at work the next morning after another night spent tossing and turning, Rafferty knew, whatever else he might be avoiding, he could no longer put off going to the mortuary to see the bodies of the murder victims.

He had deliberately put this off, reluctant to see in death the two young women who had so appealed to him in life. But it was his duty to go. How many times had he told junior officers, particularly young Smales, who was even more squeamish than Rafferty, that seeing the body of a murder victim would arm them with a determination to find the person responsible and bring them to justice?

Llewellyn had already visited the mortuary. But then Llewellyn was a strictly brought-up Methodist who had been taught never to shirk duty's demands, however unpleasant. And unpleasant he would find it, as Llewellyn had told him all about it on his return.

'What sort of person can kill a young woman like Jenny Warburton so savagely and then just shove her behind dustbins as if she was so much trash?' Llewellyn had asked, shaking his head in despair. 'The killer even scattered part of the contents of the bins over her. For added concealment? Or to degrade her after death as well as before? It didn't stop the local foxes finding her body.'

Rafferty had winced, even though, with his usual delicacy, Llewellyn refrained from elaborating on his description of Jenny's end; he didn't need to. Even without the official photographs, Rafferty's nightmares supplied, only too clearly, sufficient detail of the mutilated bodies of both Jenny and Estelle.

He blinked several times rapidly. He had been trying to put from his mind the pictures his nightmares had conjured up of the sweet and lovely Jenny ending up covered in rubbish and providing a meal for the local vermin. The forensic report indicated that she must have died almost immediately after she had walked round the corner of the

Cranstons' home to their parking area. The location of her body pointed to that conclusion as did the post-mortem hypostasis.

With savage self-accusation, Rafferty asked himself again, why didn't I walk her to her car? If I had, she'd still be alive.

'Are you feeling all right?'

Rafferty came to himself to find Llewellyn standing in front of his desk, studying him with a concerned expression. So deep in thought and self-recrimination had he been that he hadn't noticed the Welshman enter. Rafferty couldn't bring himself to ask him how he'd got on with Nigel; no doubt, if his cousin chose to drop a heavy hint or two in spite of the sizeable bribe he'd extracted, he would learn all about it soon enough.

He forced a smile and reassured Llewellyn. 'Nothing wrong with me, Daff,' he said. 'Just this case. It's a bit of a choker, isn't it?'

Silently, Llewellyn had nodded.

Since Harry Simpson had been in charge of the case when the girls' bodies had been found, Rafferty had escaped attendance at the post-mortems. But he still had to brace himself for what most would regard as the less demanding duty of the two, as he made his way to the station car park and headed for the mortuary, whipping his glasses off as soon as he had exited police premises.

* * *

The male mortuary assistant strolled along the bank of drawers, pulled out two and withdrew the concealing sheets from both bodies. 'Here are your Lonely Hearts victims, Inspector. Take a look and welcome,' he invited in a tone of black cheer that he must have caught from Sam Dally.

Rafferty managed to bite back the sharp retort. But given that he'd taken a fancy – *more* than a fancy – to the two victims, he was feeling especially sensitive. He had feared he would feel like a voyeur when he stared at their naked flesh. Thankfully, as he edged forward till he was peering into the face that the toe-tag assured him was Jenny Warburton, the fates relented and saved him from feeling this additional guilt. All he felt was the deep sadness of grief.

After hearing Simpson's and Llewellyn's descriptions, studying the scene-of-crime photographs and reading Sam Dally's PM report, he had steeled himself for the same sights in the flesh. At least he had thought he had. But he still rocked back on his heels when he saw what remained of Jenny's once-lovely face.

According to Sam's report, she had been bludgeoned with some considerable force. She had also been slashed around the face, neck and chest with a sharp knife. Neither weapon had so far been found. There was little left of the loveliness that Rafferty had so admired. Even Jenny's long, silky blonde hair had been hacked off in a final act of savagery that sickened him.

With a heavy sigh he drew the sheet back over her and, with dragging steps, made his way to the second drawer. But as he gazed down at Estelle Meredith he saw that Sam's report had been right. For although Estelle had suffered a similar attack and had her hair hacked off also, her face was still recognisable, unlike Jenny's. It was curious.

He was experienced enough to know that serial killers, if that was what they had on their hands, almost invariably became more violent with each attack, not less. Although her body hadn't been discovered till four days after her death, the post-mortem – as well as other evidence – had revealed that Jenny had been the *first* victim, not the second, so why had she been so much more brutalised than Estelle? If Llewellyn was right and their killer was a misogynist, then he loathed women so much he couldn't even bring himself to touch their flesh with his own. Certainly, whatever else he might have done, he had raped neither girl.

Rafferty gestured to the assistant that he had seen enough. He was trudging forlornly back to the car park when he heard Sam Dally 'hello' him from the other end of the long corridor. He sighed, not sure he had the stomach, in this particular case, for Sam's usual colourful humour, which, like the early Fords, was all black. He watched, teeth gritted, as the rubicund Dally bounced along the corridor towards him.

He peered into Rafferty's face. 'Wouldn't have recognised you if it hadn't been for your tired brown suit. Llewellyn told me about your new image. I have to say it's not an improvement.' Sam patted his own bald spot and added, 'You'll lose your hair naturally soon enough without anticipating it.' Thankfully, he made no further comment on Rafferty's looks and became more businesslike. 'You've been to see the two Lonely Hearts lassies, I take it?'

Rafferty nodded.

'Wondered when you'd get around to fitting it into your busy schedule.' After unleashing his first volley, which revealed with less-than-subtle irony that he had heard all about Rafferty's work-avoidance schemes, Sam quickly followed through with a second. 'So the lonely heart gets the Lonely Hearts case. Made for each other, laddie. I bet you thanked your lucky stars you missed the PMs. Lovely muscle tone on that Meredith girl. She obviously kept very fit. She was one of the healthiest corpses I've ever seen. And as for the other lassie, Jenny Warburton, she had as fine a pair of lungs on her as I've ever seen. Obviously—'

'Do you have to be quite so coarse, Sam?'

Sam stared owlishly back at him from behind his glasses and immediately rebuked Rafferty for his assumption. 'I was about to add, if you'd given me the chance, that she had obviously never smoked in her life. But even if that hadn't been what I'd intended to say, you've no business calling me names, Rafferty. Am I not surrounded by corpses all day, every day? Do you expect me to go about perpetually hung in gloom like some professional Victorian mourner?'

It would make a pleasant change, thought Rafferty. But even in his present unhappy mood, he recognised he was being unreasonable. Sam was back to his old self – *more* than his old self – after the death of his wife some months earlier. Then, Sam *had* certainly resembled a gloom-shrouded professional mourner.

So, Rafferty concluded, the rumours that Sam Dally was courting were true. It was a bitter pill that even the round and balding Dally could find love, not once, but twice. Sometimes, it seemed to Rafferty that the whole world was courting or happily paired – except him.

'What do you want, Sam?' he asked wearily. 'I've read the reports.'

'Yes, but have you *understood* 'em? I know you, Rafferty. How many times is it that I've had to break down the simplest bit of forensic science into words of one syllable for your benefit? Times without number.'

'What is there *to* understand? I've just seen the bodies. Both victims were killed where they were discovered. Or,' he added with a savagery that so surprised Dally that he took a step back, pursed his lips and studied him, 'have you saved some particularly unedifying titbit just for me?'

'Och, you're out of sorts, I can see.' Sam peered at Rafferty over his wire frames. 'You should take Sergeant Llewellyn up on his offer to fix you up with a lassie. It's plain to me you're no getting enough of something.'

How on earth had Sam Dally learned of Dafyd's offer to fix him up with this Abra girl? Surely the discreet Llewellyn hadn't taken up gossiping about his love life behind his back?

'I've been waiting for you to question me as to why Estelle Meredith, the second victim, should have been attacked with much less ferocity than the first victim. But questions came there none. Does it no strike you as curious, man?'

'Of course it does,' Rafferty replied. 'But I've not had much time to think about it.' Truth to tell, after seeing the bodies of the two girls whom he had liked so much, Rafferty was reluctant to think too deeply about anything. He was scared his nightmares would become even more terrifying if he did so. Even before they'd started, he'd been forced by circumstances to put so many of his energies into covering his tracks that he'd had little left over for the investigation.

'I'd make time, if I were you, Rafferty. It could be important.'

Rafferty nodded dumbly and made to walk away.

Behind him, Sam pshawed. 'Och, you're no fun any more, Rafferty. You used to give me a good fight even when you were feeling liverish.' After telling him he should get a doctor to look at him, Sam stalked away. But he turned back to shout after Rafferty, 'But don't ask *this* doctor to give you the once-over. You're giving such a good impression of a walking corpse I might just be tempted to open you up to see if you've finally managed to pickle your liver.'

Rafferty felt no inclination to rise to Sam's bait. Instead, with a mournful sigh that was as much for himself, the walking corpse as Sam called him, as it was for the real corpses of the two once-pretty girls lying in frozen storage in the mortuary, Rafferty left.

Nine

As he drove away from Elmhurst General after seeing the bodies of the two victims, Rafferty told himself the week could surely hold no more anguish. He hadn't reckoned on The Third Estate's contribution, but then he had rather counted on the recent outbreak of murderous gang warfare between rival asylum seekers in Habberstone, four miles to the west, to hold the front page.

So it was a shock when he rounded the corner into Bacon Lane and saw the latest placards outside the newsagents; the Lonely Hearts murders were at last hitting the headlines. And as he slowed to read some of the names the papers' editors had decided on for the killer – *The Beast*; *Sicko*; *Psycho*; *Butcher* – he found himself thanking his guardian angel that Nigel was no longer a suspect. He prayed his cousin never came back into the frame. Because if he *did*, Rafferty knew Nigel, who wasn't into such principles as honour amongst thieves or not grassing on kith and kin, would hold back no longer.

It was a huge relief for Rafferty, when he popped out later to check on the headlines, to see that another, late-breaking tragedy had forced news about the Lonely Hearts murders off the front pages of the nationals. With any luck, Nigel's alibi providing lady friends would have had little opportunity to see the quickly supplanted *'Beast'* headlines and be tempted to retract their statements.

For once, luck was on his side. It must have been because neither Kylie Smith nor Kay-leigh Jenkins contacted him. He had begun to relax a bit when, later than afternoon, Timothy Smales stuck his head round the open door of his office and asked, 'Can I see you, sir?'

After the last fraught hours, Rafferty wasn't in the mood for Smales, especially if he had come to have another whinge about the York interviews. In case this *had* been Smales's intention, Rafferty was curt with him. 'I don't know, Smales. Can you? Or is your eyesight fading, like mine? Never mind,' he added as Smales blinked uncom-prehendingly at him. 'What do you want, anyway?'

Smales came in and shut the door behind him with exaggerated care then stood in front of Rafferty's desk with an air of barely suppressed excitement. His down-covered cheeks were rosy-pink, which Rafferty had come to know meant the young officer thought he had learned something vital. He certainly looked full to bursting with something, which served to increase Rafferty's heart rate and feeling of impending doom. And when he learned what it was, he could only stare at the constable, appalled.

At any other time, Rafferty would have commended the young man standing so triumphantly before him and expecting the praise he thought his due. He would have been pleased Smales was at last showing some maturity and had begun to grow into his chosen career. Only why did he have to choose *now*, of all times, to start to show some initiative?

When the praise failed to materialise, Smales at first looked puzzled. But his puzzlement was soon replaced by a return to the sulky schoolboy routine that had accompanied them back from York.

With a trace of belligerence, he said to Rafferty, 'I thought you'd be pleased. You're always going on about the need to show initiative. Sir.'

This 'sir' was thrown in as a sop to authority, Rafferty could tell. But if he was to avoid Smales sharing the tale about his unethical conduct in York with the entire nick he would have to ignore the dumb insolence and instead of the stick of reprimand, offer the carrot compliment.

'I *am* pleased,' Rafferty told him, through

gritted teeth. 'You've done well, very well.' *Too* bloody well, he silently added. Maybe if he'd troubled to soothe Smales's ego earlier, the young officer wouldn't have taken it upon himself to ring both Kylie Smith and Kayleigh Jenkins to recheck their alibis. Of course, during these conversations, Smales had revealed the very thing Rafferty had been at pains to keep from them: that Nigel Blythe had been their main *suspect* rather than the innocent victim of a targeted burglary as Rafferty had implied.

As he had feared and as Smales jauntily confirmed, informed of the true situation, the two women hadn't been able to retract their alibis quickly enough.

He hadn't anticipated the sudden and untimely show of initiative. But it was too late now and Rafferty applied his mind to damage limitation.

Mollified after Rafferty's effusive compliments, Smales remarked, 'It's strange, isn't it, sir, that they should both have somehow got hold of the wrong end of the stick about Nigel Blythe?'

'Mm,' Rafferty agreed. 'Wonder how they could have got such an idea?' Even as he posed the question, he suspected the newly-inspired Smales would be able to enlighten him. And so it proved.

'I asked them about it,' Smales revealed, 'and they both said that *you'd* told them.'

'They did?' Rafferty put on what he hoped was a convincing show of bewilderment. He shook his head more in sorrow than anger at the vagaries of human nature. 'But then, when you've had as much experience as I have of the behaviour of witnesses, you'll realise what a contradictory lot they can be. Not only do they not listen properly, they change their stories at the drop of a hat. They're not to be relied upon, Smales. If you learn nothing more than that during your early police career, you'll be doing very well.'

Even as he tried to muddy the waters of Smales's evidence, Rafferty was struck by the horrified realisation that it had only been the fact of his 'solid' alibis that had stopped Nigel from dropping him in it. And now, thanks to Smales's untimely show of initiative, Nigel *had* no alibis...

His judgement had slipped badly and he set out to retrieve something from a situation that could turn out to be a real danger to both himself and Nigel. He managed to divert Smales's suspicions and sympathies on to a different track entirely, by saying to him, 'We only have the word of two women who've shown they're unreliable. They're both married women, Smales. Does it not cross your mind that after speaking to you they were more worried about their husbands learning about their adultery than they were about Nigel Blythe's future? How would you feel if your name was smeared in the paper before you had a chance to prove your innocence?'

Put like that, Smales admitted he would feel outraged.

'So would I. So, for the time being I want you to say nothing to anyone about these alibi retractions. Leave it to me to consider the best interests of all concerned, including Nigel Blythe. Okay?'

Even though Smales gave a conspiratorial nod at this, Rafferty hadn't much faith in Smales's silence lasting. But just as long as it lasted till he'd found the murderer, he would ask no more.

'The two ladies said they'd phone you and retract officially, like.'

Rafferty nodded. He didn't doubt it. As if on cue, his phone began to ring.

After Rafferty had dismissed Smales, he had listened with a fatalistic air as, in turn, Mesdames Smith and Jenkins explained that of course they hadn't been thinking about the effect on their marriages when they had told the young officer they wanted to withdraw their alibis. No, they had realised it was their public duty to tell the truth now they understood that Nigel Blythe might be a dangerous criminal. It was the thought of Nigel stalking the streets looking for further victims that had prompted their attacks of conscience and their decision to tell the truth, not any concern for their own marital accord. Nigel *hadn't* been with them at all, both women insisted. They hadn't even seen him since shortly after lunch on either day.

Naturally, Rafferty – who had been clinging to the wreckage of his cousin's alibis – hadn't wanted to believe them. He had been blunt with both women. 'So, now, in spite of your previous statement,' he challenged Kylie Smith, 'you're denying that you and Nigel spent the entire evening together on Friday, the 4th of April?'

'I most certainly am.'

Rafferty could picture Kylie Smith at the other end of the phone, shaking her bleached blonde curls indignantly

'I'm a *professional*, Inspector,' Mrs Smith had insisted. 'My firm paid for me to go to that delightful post-modern hotel for training purposes, not to pick up men. After spending no more than half an hour, if that, in Nigel's room, I went to my own and studied the training literature. That would have been around 2.30 in the afternoon. I didn't see Nigel again after that.'

And from this stance, she wasn't to be shifted. Neither was Kayleigh Jenkins who took a line so similar about Nigel's alibi for the Saturday night they might have practised it together. Perhaps they had. The only good aspect about the two telephone interviews was that they hadn't been overheard. It meant he would be able, for a while anyway, to conceal from his cousin – and the super and the rest of the team – that Nigel's alibis were worthless. Such a revelation would quickly propel his cousin into 'telling all', something he had to avoid at all costs.

Even though he had been unwilling to believe the women were now telling the truth, such had been the conviction in their voices that Rafferty was forced to the unwelcome conclusion that Nigel's alibis really were as worthless as they claimed.

So where *had* Nigel been? More to the point – what had he been doing and why had he lied about it?

It was only then that a possibility occurred to Rafferty that he had never before considered. If, as he believed, the two women were now telling the truth, Nigel could have had ample time to drive back to Elmhurst from York. He even knew where the parties were being held, as Rafferty had mentioned it when he had telephoned him on his mobile to thank him again for his help.

Was it possible he'd been doing his best to shield Nigel and remove him entirely as chief suspect when all the time his cousin *had* been guilty of the brutal murders of the two women?

He found it hard to believe. Nigel might be

a bit of a rogue where money, deals and women were concerned, but surely he wasn't into murderous violence as well? Still, the possibility stunned him so much that he was at a loss what to do next. If he challenged Nigel about his failed alibis, his cousin, who had been the soul of discretion thus far, albeit in return for Rafferty paying him some not inconsiderable sums, would, if innocent, feel so outraged he would sing like a caged canary.

Rafferty knew he had no choice but to suppress the knowledge of the alibis' retraction. Apart from himself, Smales was the only one who knew the truth and he'd been silenced for the moment.

Alone in his office, Rafferty had too many moments to consider the inevitable repercussions should Smales fail to meet this discretion test. Rafferty knew he would be exposed, reviled and probably caged himself.

He put his head in his hands and breathed out on a long, shuddering sigh. After everything else, the thought of being hauled before the beak courtesy of little Timmy Smales, of all people, was too much to bear.

While his troubles multiplied, Rafferty was comforted by the thought that at least he was still managing to avoid meeting the main witnesses. He didn't know how much longer he would be able to achieve the trick, but fortunately, Llewellyn, who had at first kept harping on about it, had quickly resigned himself to doing the bulk of the interviews.

This acceptance had surprised Rafferty, but he was too grateful to question it. But, although he kept well away from anyone with any connection to the Made In Heaven dating agency, the nightmares pushed Rafferty into an even more assiduous study of all the reports and witness statements as they came in. He read them over and over as if they were Holy Writ, sure there must be something there that would start the grit in the oyster of his memory. He had been there, he reminded himself again, as if a reminder was necessary. He *must* have the pre-knowledge that would point him to the solution of the case.

But, of course, at both parties he had been doing his best to keep his policeman persona under wraps. He had been so concerned with keeping up his accent and his corner and keeping down his alcohol intake and his dropped aitches that he had been fully occupied. Even so, he thought, surely there must be *something* in all this vast pile of verbiage?

But if there was something, Rafferty hadn't been able to find it, with or without his father's glasses. The continuing headaches didn't help, of course. Now he had the nightmare induced sleepless nights to contend with also.

His uncharacteristic devotion to paperwork had, early in the investigation, brought the inevitable observation from Llewellyn that this case seemed to have sparked a marked change of character in Rafferty. Rafferty had taken this to mean he wasn't being his usual cavalier self in his attitude to paperwork, and he had warned himself to be careful and indulge his feverish study of the reports only when Llewellyn was absent from the station. But with so much else to think about, Rafferty knew he hadn't managed that particular essential too well.

Strangely, however, Llewellyn had made no further comment about it, which was pretty uncharacteristic of *him*. Rafferty couldn't help but wonder why this should be. Although he was aware that Llewellyn thought him mercurial, he had no reason to think him so mercurial that he would change the habits of a lifetime so completely.

And then there was another thing that puzzled him. Although they still occasionally had the spats which had characterised their early days of working together, their differences had been mostly set aside and they had turned into a good team. At least they *had*, before this case had put Rafferty under such a strain. He was basically too honest –

too simple – a man to find living a lie easy. It made him hit out – no doubt from Llewellyn's point of view – unfairly.

But oddly, Llewellyn failed to retaliate in his previous superior manner. Instead, he would go silent. It was almost as if Llewellyn was making allowances for behaviour that Rafferty couldn't help. Occasionally, Rafferty would catch Llewellyn looking at him with something close to pity in his eyes. And, much to his irritation, Llewellyn would try again to bring up the subject of matchmaking Rafferty with this Abra woman.

Rafferty suspected that Llewellyn, newly come to wedded bliss, increasingly regarded him as some poor, lovelorn creature who, if left to his own resources, would be doomed to a solitary life. And when he was forced to think again about the poor savaged bodies of Jenny and Estelle, he began to believe Llewellyn might be right.

By dint of desperation and ingenuity, Rafferty had managed to divert Smales's suspicions and obtain his *omertà* promise. That left the two women. But, he felt reasonably confident that his threat to charge them would be sufficient deterrent to further probing when Nigel remained unarrested.

After the latest fraught experience in a fraught-filled week, Rafferty felt he was entitled to think the day could hold no more punishing surprises. But he had thought without his own particular *bête noire*, Superintendent Bradley.

For, twenty minutes after he'd got off the phone to Nigel's ex-alibis, he learned that Smales's revelation wasn't the last of the day's traumas.

He had just reached for the latest reports and begun to settle down in an attempt to absorb them when the phone rang. And, as he discovered, his caller wasn't in the best of tempers.

'What's this I hear?' Superintendent Bradley's bluff, gruff Yorkshire tones bellowed in Rafferty's ear.

Warily, he replied, 'I don't know, Super. What is it you hear?'

'Don't come the mimic with me, Rafferty. From what I've just learned, you're in no position to act the smart alec.'

The hairs on the back of Rafferty's neck rose up in alarm at this. *What* had Bradley heard? Surely even Smales couldn't have blabbed already?

Ten

Only too aware that Bradley was capable of baiting a trap and waiting to see what fell in, Rafferty was wary. 'I don't know what you mean, sir,' he said.

'Allow me to enlighten you. Dereliction of duty is what I mean. Correct me if I'm wrong, but it *was* you I put in charge of the Lonely Hearts murders?' Obviously, this was a rhetorical question, because Bradley didn't wait for a reply. 'Only it seems that Sergeant Llewellyn's running it and doing nearly all of the vital witness interviews. What's going on, Rafferty? Bottle gone since Llewellyn stole your thunder on your last investigation?'

'No, sir.'

'You do want to solve this case, I take it?'

'Of course I do, sir.' And how. 'But there was a lot to do and I had to prioritise. Amongst other things, I felt it was vital I check out this Nigel Blythe's alibis, which involved travelling up to York. It's not as if Sergeant Llewellyn isn't more than capable of conducting the important initial interviews. As you yourself said, sir, he did solve our last case. I have every faith in him.'

'Coming from a lapsed Catholic who presumably has damned little faith in anything, that's not comforting, Rafferty. I want to see more active involvement from your good self. See that I do.'

The receiver banged down. Fortunately, Rafferty, used to his chief's penchant for reverberating exits, had removed his ear just in time. 'Yes, sir,' he muttered to the empty office. 'Should I arrest myself now or would you prefer me to suffer on for a while longer?'

But whatever else he did, it was clear he could no longer avoid the main witnesses. Still undecided about what action to take on the Nigel front, Bradley's order at least aided decision on one aspect. It also served as a reminder that his performance in his last investigation had done little to enhance his reputation. It made it doubly unfortunate that he should be so hog-tied in this case. He needed results, not only to give the two dead girls justice and save his own hide and Nigel's, but also – supposing by some miracle he managed such a quiverful of tricks – to ensure Bradley wouldn't have another failure with which to beat him.

At least Llewellyn would have no further call to wonder about his uncharacteristically dutiful study of the witnesses' statements. And as his new cousin-by-marriage had long since taken his measure, he was thankful to have one small mercy in his sea of troubles.

The following morning, after he woke, sluggish from yet another nightmare, Rafferty thought his spirit could sink no further. But then he recalled the day's duties and almost pulled the duvet back over his head. But he forced himself out.

On arrival at the station Rafferty briskly informed Llewellyn that this time they were both to visit the agency. Even now, with his choice of action limited by Bradley's order, his feet dragged as they approached the agency's Hope Street offices. The arrow-clutching rosy cherubs peering out from their clouds above the shop front seemed to gaze at him with reproachful eyes. Somehow, Rafferty forced himself to follow Llewellyn through the doorway.

He was surprised to find that Isobel Goddard hadn't taken off for her parents' home again, but was seated behind her desk in reception. At their entrance her head jerked apprehensively upwards. And even when Llewellyn moved closer so her short-sighted eyes could recognise him, the apprehension lingered. As Isobel squinted in Rafferty's direction, his heart started up such a wild beating he thought it might leap out of his chest. He had taken the precaution of remaining near the door, out of her field of vision, and he felt a hot, sweaty relief when, without a flicker of recognition, her attention returned to Llewellyn.

'Not you again?' she asked.

'I'm afraid so, Miss Goddard,' Llewellyn replied. 'I've brought Inspector Rafferty with me this time. He wanted to ask you some questions.'

Isobel pouted and spared Rafferty a myopic glance. 'It's taken him long enough. I suppose you expect me to repeat my statement yet again? How many more times must I—?'

'As often as necessary,' Rafferty told her in a deliberately deepened voice that brought a narrowing of Llewellyn's gaze. 'Surely I don't have to remind you that two young women have been murdered? I would have thought you would be only too anxious to help us catch the person responsible.' He paused, wary of saying more, in case something in his voice betrayed him. But when another pout was her only response, he was emboldened to continue. 'I have some questions about Estelle Meredith. Can you tell me how long she had been on your books?'

Isobel shrugged. 'Several months. She dated practically every halfway decent male we can offer.'

Her tone indicated her resentment of the fact. Rafferty got the impression that Isobel regarded the more affluent male clients as her private fiefdom and resented the competition; but given what he had already heard about her, this didn't come as a surprise. 'But,' he began, before he stopped abruptly as he realised he had been about to reveal that Estelle had said she had only joined the agency the previous week and had had few dates. Of course, as Nigel, he knew that, but as the investigating policeman, he couldn't know. For God's sake, Rafferty, he rebuked himself, try to remember. If Isobel Goddard was to be believed, Estelle hadn't been entirely honest with him. But then she was in good company...

'But?' Isobel repeated. 'But what?'

Rafferty, tired of being pulled up every time he uttered a one-word objection, managed to come up with a plausible response. 'But I understood from the statements that very few of the other members admit to going out with her.'

'They would, wouldn't they, given that she's been murdered? But it's true enough, because most of the ones who did are no longer on our books. Not that I'm suggesting that Estelle Meredith scared them off.' She frowned and added, 'Though she did flirt outrageously. She seemed to be out to prove something.'

'Like what?'

Isobel shrugged. 'That she was attractive to men, I suppose. I got the impression with

Estelle that she wasn't nearly as confident as she made out.'

'Like much of the rest of humanity.' Rafferty paused. 'There was one other matter I wanted to ask you about. I understand you were concerned you might have been the murderer's intended victim. I wondered if there was a particular reason why you should think so.'

Isobel became defensive. 'No, not really. It was just a feeling I had, that's all. You know, that feeling that someone's walked over your grave?'

It was a feeling Rafferty had lately become familiar with. 'So you've no *particular* reason to think you might have been the intended target?'

'I told you, no.' Isobel's hands formed into white-knuckled fists where they rested on the desk and, as though conscious of their capacity for betrayal, she lowered them to her lap, out of sight. 'I just became scared, as anyone would.'

Rafferty could think of no more questions he could safely ask Isobel that didn't risk him revealing something else he wasn't supposed to know. Instead, he asked if Simon Farnell or Caroline Durward were in.

Isobel nodded. 'Simon is. But Caroline's working at home today.' She made no attempt to use the intercom to alert Simon Farnell to their presence; instead, she got up from behind her desk with something approaching alacrity and made for the hallway where the private offices were situated. Her 'I'll tell Simon you want to see him' floated behind her as she vanished from sight.

While they waited, Llewellyn picked up one of the magazines from a table, began to flick through it and was soon immersed.

Rafferty was glad Llewellyn was occupied. It gave him some thinking time. Again it struck him that he and the killer might not be the only ones with guilty secrets. Isobel's defensive manner, her alacrity in pushing them and their questions on to Simon Farnell indicated she, too, might have something to hide.

Only now did he recall that on the night of the first party, Isobel had followed Jenny Warburton from the Cranstons' drawing room. Was it merely coincidence? Or had she followed Jenny deliberately?

By the time he had managed to push his way through the throng she had been halfway across the hallway. Had Isobel veered in the direction of the Ladies' only when she became aware of his presence behind her? He couldn't be sure; as the case progressed, the more hazy his memory became and badgering it only made it hazier. He put it down to stress. But at least, early in the case, he had retained sufficient of his Nigel persona recollections to prime

Llewellyn with appropriate questions. The statements revealed that another guest had also noticed Isobel's exit immediately after Jenny. Questioned about it, Isobel had said she had wanted to get away from a bore and repair her make-up, which Rafferty acknowledged was plausible. From his fading recollections of Bliss's party gossip, it fitted her character. If she *hadn't* been following Jenny, she might well have spotted a better prospect over the bore's shoulder and been intent on doing some running repairs to her make-up made necessary by the steamy weather.

Another vague impression swam into his memory – that on his return from saying goodbye to Jenny the door to the Ladies' had been ajar. Isobel could have listened to their conversation, heard him return and enter the Gents' and realised that Jenny had set off to the car park alone. She could have followed only a few seconds behind, collecting previously hidden weapons and protective clothing on the way, and taken Jenny by surprise with the first blow.

But what possible motive could the girl have? Admittedly, she seemed to regard the more wealthy of the male clientele as her private harem. In addition, according to Bliss, Isobel carried a wealth of family expectation on her back. But surely, the family pressure, even with the ruthless Elizabethan forebear providing an example of how to deal with love rivals, would be insufficient to prompt her to remove the competition permanently?

Even to Rafferty, who was often given to flights of fancy, such a possibility seemed far-fetched. Apart from anything else, it was doubtful if Isobel had the brains to get away with murder. Not that such a lack would necessarily stop her trying. Rafferty paused, mid-thought. Was Isobel *really* as dim and shallow as she appeared or was it a protective façade? What had the statement that Llewellyn had taken from her parents' garrulous neighbour said about her? That it was *sad how she had changed.* That was it. That *she used to be such a bright little thing, nose always in a book. Now, she's just man mad. Her life's an endless round of partying. Where has the child gone, I wonder, who used to watch the stars with me on clear summer nights and ask such intelligent questions?*

Where indeed? Rafferty thought. Had Isobel been hiding the light of her intelligence under a bushel of coquetry because she believed men still feared intelligent women? Or was the concealment done for more sinister reasons?

Isobel had presented herself as being too dim to get away with murder. She had even returned to her parents' home, leaving the impression behind that she was scared she might be the killer's real target. But if she wasn't so dim after all, her flight home could have been an attempt to cover her tracks.

He was beginning to wonder why it was taking Isobel so long to inform Simon Farnell of their presence in reception when Farnell came out and ushered them into his office and Rafferty had to put any further speculation aside.

'What can I do for you, Inspector?' Farnell asked after Llewellyn had made the introductions and they had all sat down around his desk.

'I just wanted to ask a few more questions, sir. I was surprised to see Miss Goddard back in the office. You told my officers she believed she might have been the murderer's intended target. Strange she should have returned at all, especially to work at the very agency which has had two members killed.'

Simon Farnell smiled. 'Unfathomable are the ways of women, Inspector. Or so I've always found. But then I've never thought Isobel terribly bright. I imagine her mother convinced her she was being stupid, put some backbone and much-needed sense into her and persuaded her back to work.'

Baulked of a satisfactory explanation from Isobel, Rafferty persisted. 'Have you any idea why Miss Goddard should think she might have been the intended target? Had she been threatened in some way?'

'If she had, she didn't mention it to me. But Isobel's a bit of a drama queen, Inspector. If attention isn't revolving round her she's prone to do or say something outrageous to encourage it.' Farnell shrugged. 'I wouldn't take anything Isobel says too seriously. As you yourself said – she's back. So how worried could she have been? And as I told her, if someone *did* want to kill her, they would have to be singularly inept to make a botch of it not once but twice. Besides, even Isobel's capable of concluding that she's unlikely to find a rich husband while she's buried at home in the country, especially as her family no longer have the money to entertain.'

Rafferty leaned back in his chair and tried for nonchalance. Lancelot Bliss had said something similar. 'You surprise me. You'd never think it to look at Miss Goddard.' He straightened his off-the-peg and increasingly shabby brown jacket and remarked self-deprecatingly, 'Of course I'm just a male plod and pretty ignorant about such things, as the female members of my family frequently tell me, but Miss Goddard's suit looked suspiciously like a designer one to me.'

From the corner of his eye Rafferty caught another startled glance from the designer-suited Llewellyn, who well knew the extent of his inspector's ignorance in matters sartorial. He shrugged aside Llewellyn's reaction, keen to learn as much officially about the party guests as 'Nigel' had, so as to lessen the risk of revealing prior knowledge. And as Simon Farnell appeared to be as avid a gossip as Lancelot Bliss, this was a prime opportunity.

Farnell smiled. 'You've a good eye, Inspector. Isobel's suit *is* designer. But it's true the family hasn't a bean.' He told them this with a certain relish. 'Rumour has it that some foolish speculative venture did for them financially just before Isobel entered her teens. They've been on their uppers ever since. Every penny they have is put on Isobel's back. I gather she's meant to be the human sacrifice that placates the gods and puts everything right.'

'Human sacrifice?' Rafferty echoed.

'Isobel's supposed to sacrifice herself on some rich man's altar, snare herself said husband and so restore the family fortunes.'

'I thought stuff like that went out with the Victorians.'

Farnell laughed. 'Don't you believe it, Inspector. Persuading a nubile daughter to sacrifice herself for the sake of the family is still pretty rife, at least amongst the upper elements of society. Hasn't the aristocracy a reputation for ruthlessness in pursuit of their desires? Not that Isobel's unwilling, far from it. That's the trouble. For all that she's from a real “true blue” blackground, Isobel’s vamp routine’s been borrowed from the Mae West school of seduction. It gives the agency a bad image, as I’ve several times complained to Caroline. Of course, as far as the agency’s concerned, the sacrifice of the not-so-nubile daughters can be lucrative. We get a lot of business from fathers of plain, middle-class girls past the first flush egged-on by mothers who want grandchildren before it’s too late. We have a sideline in makeovers and have an arrangement with a first-class plastic surgeon who’s also joint owner of a beauty salon, so we’re able to quickly arrange for a bit of plastic surgery, boob jobs, laser eye treatment, Botox, etc. After all that, mummy and daddy have a real chance of wedding bells and babies. Demeaning for the girls to realise that even their parents believe they have no hope of hooking a worthy man without such measures. I feel sorry for them sometimes.’

So did Rafferty. And to think he hadn’t even clipped his nasal hair before climbing into his ill-fitting borrowed suit and entering the agency dating ring. ‘And you say that Isobel’s willing to do whatever’s necessary?’

‘Why wouldn’t she be? Isobel would like a return to the good life as much as the rest of her family. She’s already had a boob job – you might have noticed she has plenty to put in the shop window. I gather she’s speedily amassing funds to have her short sight corrected. She's paying for the operations herself, too. God knows where she gets the money as her salary's not large.'

Rafferty was beginning to have one or two ideas about that.

'You won't know this, of course, having just met the girl' – was that another hint of criticism? Rafferty wondered, aware he was becoming sensitive to such sly rebukes – 'but she's not only dim and not very efficient, she's also lazy and indiscreet – not the best secretary/receptionist from the agency's point of view, which is something else I've been at pains to make clear to Caroline.'

Rafferty wanted a few moments to think, so he signalled to Llewellyn to take over. Farnell certainly seemed to have a down on Isobel. Was that just because he was clearly homosexual and Isobel's crass style offended his own impeccable taste? Or was there a deeper reason? Lancelot Bliss had revealed that Isobel was a bit of a snoop. Did she have something unsavoury on Farnell? But given that Farnell made no secret of his homosexuality, what *could* she have on him? Isobel would be unable to use her usual weapon – her body – to prise his secrets from him, as some of the recent statements hinted she did.

Llewellyn had discovered that Farnell had pushed to set up a 'gay' section to the dating agency and although Guy Cranston had made no objection, Caroline *had*. Was it possible that *Farnell* was the killer but that he had mistakenly killed the wrong women? Given that Caroline had crushed his ambition by rejecting out of hand his desire to set up the gay section and if Isobel *did* have some kind of hold on him, either woman could have been his chosen victim.

If so and Farnell had made a botch of it, his remark that such a killer would have to be completely inept to make such a mistake not once, but twice, could be a double-bluff.

'You're looking very thoughtful, Inspector. I do hope you're not judging me too harshly for my frank comments about Isobel.' Simon Farnell gave him a coy glance from under his lashes.

Rafferty assumed the man must have a taste for the butch look he currently sported. Dear God, he thought, please don't let him start *flirting* with me. Not on top of all my other troubles. I might just land him one.

'Just so you don't think I'm being a spiteful queen, let me give you an instance of Isobel's ineptitude. The party where we've since learned Jenny Warburton was murdered was another of her muddles. She caused both Caroline and me to arrive late. We didn't realise until we got to The Elmhurst hotel and found there was no booking that Isobel had given us invitations for the previous week's function. It wasn't the first time something like that has happened, either. I can only think Caroline puts up with her because it was Guy who took her on.' Simon sighed. 'The perils of nepotism.'

Rafferty recalled Simon and Caroline's late arrival at the first party; now he knew the reason for it.

'I wish Isobel *would* find herself a wealthy man to keep her in style.' Farnell looked archly at Rafferty. 'Wouldn't mind one myself, come to that.'

Beside Rafferty, his sergeant was emitting strange muffled sounds. He ignored them and observed stiltedly, 'Isobel's plan doesn't seem to be working. I gather she's been on the staff since the agency opened. How old is she, twenty-seven?' Farnell nodded. 'So what's she doing wrong?'

'As I said, Inspector, I find the female of the species unfathomable. But you're a red-blooded male, my dear, what do you think she's doing wrong?'

Rafferty winced at the 'my dear'. Careful to call to mind only Isobel's office clothing of low-cut blouse and scarlet lipstick rather than her barely-there party dress, Rafferty shrugged. 'She's a bit obvious, I suppose. Shows a bit too much flesh and wears too much make-up. It hints at desperation.'

'Perhaps you should tell her that. Then we might get her married off before she tries her vampish tricks on any more clients. Several have complained about her. She's also inclined to be inquisitive, which doesn't go down too well. Our clients expect discretion. It's the reason they come to us in the first place.'

There was no question now that Farnell had a definite down on Isobel. But as Rafferty recalled the comments in the statements of some of the male members, perhaps Farnell had a point.

'Isobel's a bit of a snoop,' Lancelot Bliss had said. *'Caught her going through my desk once. I often work at home and keep lots of confidential stuff there. Luckily, I keep the confidential stuff in a locked drawer. God knows what she was looking for.'*

'Isobel's a bit of a bike' – this had been Ralph Dryden's comment. *'Most of the members here have had a ride or two on her.'*

'Isobel likes expensive presents,' Rory Gifford had revealed.

Tired of trying and failing to find a rich husband, had Isobel settled for expensive trinkets and a sideline career as a blackmailer? Could that be why she made her body available to rich men who might have a murky secret or ten? Men forgot to be discreet when their trousers were down and their passion was up. If she *was* into using her body to encourage men to reveal their secrets it would explain why she had thought herself the murderer's intended target.

The fact that Jenny, Estelle and Isobel were all superficially alike, all being blondes, around the same height and build and all favoured little black dresses, increased the possibility of mistaken identity. In the sparsely illuminated car parking area at the Cranstons' home and the equally dimly lit rear grounds of The Elmhurst's annexe it would have been easy to mistake one girl for another.

Rafferty mentioned the possibility to Llewellyn when they left the agency offices and were back in the car. Llewellyn had taken to being the driver as quickly as he had taken to running most of the investigation. Rafferty was beginning to suspect that if he ever managed to divest himself of the shackles tying his hands in this case, he might find himself permanently in the passenger seat in more ways than one.

'After all,' he said, 'why should she think she might have been the intended victim if she didn't harbour a guilty secret or two?'

'Such a possibility had occurred to me, sir,' Llewellyn told him. 'I put something similar in my last report if you recall. I can't think how you missed it as you've been studying the paperwork so assiduously.'

Rafferty couldn't think how he'd missed it, either. He supposed he could put it down to his father's glasses. The headaches were now getting pretty insupportable. Obviously, he couldn't tell Llewellyn this. Instead, he clutched at a dim memory. 'Must be that bang on the head that's affecting my recollection.'

'What bang on the head?'

'Happened when you were on honeymoon.'

'Ah,' said Llewellyn.

'What do you mean, *Ah*?'

'Just that it would explain a lot.' Llewellyn briefly studied him, before he returned his attention to the road. 'You've been subdued lately, not like yourself. Not like yourself at all,' the usually eloquent Welshman repeated. 'You've been behaving, well, as I said, not like yourself.' Solicitously, he asked, 'Are you feeling unwell?'

Rafferty, seeing the genuine concern on Llewellyn's face, felt a brief temptation to 'tell all'. Fortunately it passed. But he was hungry for sympathy, so he decided to seize the moment and the ready excuse for his recent uncharacteristic behaviour. He made his voice weak and lacking in conviction. 'I'm all right, really. I suppose.' His pathetic reply brought the desired response.

'You're not, though, are you? Even Maureen said she's never seen you so subdued. Why not tell Dr Llewellyn what the problem is?'

The normally dour, dry-as-a-desert

Llewellyn must be worried to make such a naff effort at humour, Rafferty realised. I'm not lying, he told his nagging conscience before it got into its stride, as he confessed: 'I haven't been sleeping well. Apart from these headaches, I keep getting recurring nightmares.'

'Nightmares?' Llewellyn echoed again. 'What about?'

Rafferty was again tempted to confide his troubles to Llewellyn and put himself out of his misery. But again the temptation lasted only a moment. He could imagine Llewellyn's reaction if he told him his nightmares consisted of bloody visions, with him in the role of double murderer. So he temporised. 'I keep getting nightmares about murdering Ma.' Well, that was true, too. He *had* sometimes had murderous thoughts in that direction. He was only human. But the knowledge that his ma always bested him had put a stop to such dreams. He had never managed to win an argument with her, never mind a struggle to the death.

'There's nothing else troubling you?'

Rafferty was quick to deny it.

'Then, apart from making an appointment with your doctor for a check-up, I suggest you need a holiday. You should try to get away when we've resolved this case. A long break from murder is probably exactly what you need.'

Rafferty merely nodded, smiled and said, 'You're probably right.' It was the possibility that he'd have a very long break – an involuntary one, courtesy of Her Majesty – that had exacerbated the nightmares. But, of course, he said nothing about that. Keen to get all the most problematic interviews over as quickly as possible, he simply suggested Llewellyn put his foot down – a request sure to encourage the suddenly chatty Welshman into stubborn silence.

He made use of the journey time to think about another possibility. Thus far, because the two victims had been young women and Simon Farnell clearly played from another sexual song sheet, he hadn't featured strongly as a suspect. But the murders were not necessarily crimes of gender. Neither girl had been raped. They might well have been killed for reasons other than sexual ones.

Farnell was ambitious, gossipy and also a little spiteful. Caroline had thwarted his ambitions to launch a homosexual arm to the agency. She, rather than Guy, had been the stumbling block to this ambition. Had he tried to remove this stumbling block and made a hash of it both times?

It seemed pretty unlikely, even though the three women – Jenny, Estelle and Caroline – were superficially alike and might be confused for one another in dimly lit grounds by a man blinded by ambition. But what made the possibility difficult to accept was Farnell himself. The man might harbour ambitions, but they were realistic ones. Or they would have been if Caroline hadn't been so set against them. Farnell's resentment about this had come across clearly in his statement even though he'd barely referred to the matter. But he'd clearly researched the market. Lancelot Bliss had confided to Llewellyn that Farnell had paid for a firm of accountants to do the costings out of his own pocket. Clearly, he must be convinced his planned agency arm would meet a need.

Rafferty was inclined to agree with him; not every male homosexual would be happy to explore the more sordid ways of finding a partner. Farnell's ambition was far from blind. It was clear sighted, unhampered by distorting blinkers. That was why Rafferty had managed to convince himself that if Simon Farnell meant to kill a particular person he wouldn't mistake their identity.

There again, Isobel had managed to head him off when it came to questions about her intelligence, so maybe Farnell had done the same but from the opposite direction. Perhaps, for all Farnell's apparently intelligent application to providing solid evidence to support his desired gay section 'baby', it only pointed to what an obsession it had become to him. It didn't necessarily mean he would be able to apply such intelligence to other areas.

Given the electronic gates at New Hall, the odds were short on Jenny's murderer being one of the attendees at the house party, so he couldn't discount Farnell. Nor could he be discounted when it came to Estelle's murder as the side entrance to The Elmhurst's annexe had a spring-loaded lock that only opened from inside. So again, without complicity from someone inside, no stranger could have gained easy access to the grounds to kill Estelle.

Everyone had been questioned as to whether they had let someone in from outside; naturally, all had denied it. Nor could an outsider have gained access from the front of the annexe. Doormen had been on duty all evening to keep out potential gatecrashers.

By now, thanks to Llewellyn's diligence, most of the attendees at both parties had been whittled from the suspect list. They had already checked and disproved the possibility that a stray stranger-killer could have gained access to the first party by waiting outside the grounds of New Hall for the gates to open so he could slip through and find a girl to kill. The possibility had been there for a time; even though he had thought it too bizarre to be given any credence, his increasing paranoia had insisted he consider it. But that worry had died an early death on the study of the video footage. The camera on the gates of New Hall had failed to record any suspicious-looking characters – apart from himself – as he and Llewellyn had discovered on playing the tape back.

Rafferty had cringed when he had recognised himself in the back of the cab behind the concealing handkerchief. He had cringed even more when Llewellyn had said, 'I don't know why, but there's something strangely familiar about that cab passenger. I wish I could put my finger on what it is.'

Fortunately, Llewellyn hadn't mentioned the matter again, so Rafferty concluded his sergeant's finger had failed to find the spot. Even I must have one stroke of good fortune, Rafferty told himself.

Eleven

Next on the list was Rory Gifford, the TV producer friend of Dr Lancelot Bliss. Gifford's apartment, like Nigel's, was another of the recent developments that attracted affluent young professionals. Of course, Elmhurst was a handy commuter ride into the centre of London.

Situated on Elmhurst's outskirts, on the north bank of the river at Tiffey Reach, within easy walking distance of Northgate and the High Street with their shops and restaurants, Gifford's apartment was in a futuristic modern block. Rafferty guessed it must have stunning views over the water and the mostly open country to the north-east of the town. Each apartment had a large balcony featuring intricate ironwork and supported by metal pillars.

An entry-phone system was in operation. Rafferty pressed the button for Gifford's apartment and they were admitted to a spacious entrance hall carpeted in a soft grey and filled with huge plants lit from a central atrium. Two lifts faced the entrance door, while, to the left, a wide staircase curved round the wall.

Rafferty headed for the stairs. He'd always understood that independent TV producers led a hand-to-mouth existence. Seemed Gifford was the exception. Still, Llewellyn's research had revealed that the TV Doctor programme which featured Gifford's friend Lance Bliss was very successful. According to the rather smug statement Gifford had made which confirmed Llewellyn's research, it had sold to a number of foreign countries, including the States.

Gifford's apartment was on the second floor, not penthouse class, but as Gifford let them in and Rafferty glanced around, he concluded that it was still seriously pricey. Seriously stylish, too, in the minimalist way that Llewellyn admired, though to Rafferty, envious though he was about the large balcony, the enormous living room looked practically bare. A vast, almost cinema-size screen filled most of one wall; beneath it were assorted DVDs and video recorders. A long, black leather sofa faced the screen and in front of it was a sleek metal and glass coffee table with an assortment of zappers. Apart from a dining table large enough to seat a dozen, a couple of enormous black armchairs and ceiling-high racks holding books and yet more videos and DVDs, that was it.

As they sat on the sofa, Lancelot Bliss appeared clutching a mug of coffee. He greeted them in his TV Doctor voice as if they were nervous guests on his programme who had to be put at their ease.

'Come in, come in,' he said, as if he owned the place. 'Make yourselves at home. I always do.' He sat down in one of the easy chairs and sprawled back as if determined to show how much at ease he was even when, as now, he was a suspect in a murder enquiry.

Lancelot Bliss was undoubtedly an actor *manqué*. The female members of the dating agency, so Rafferty had learned after suggesting Llewellyn ask around, tended to like him and forgave him his vanity. The men, particularly the older ones, generally considered him something of a popinjay, though an amusing one. Perhaps surprisingly, he was considered a first-rate doctor, though that might simply be the result of expensive PR.

Bliss again wore the exquisite fob watch that Rafferty had noticed at the first party. He guessed it was a favourite piece and showy enough to satisfy the doctor for he drew it out and consulted it at regular intervals, either to show it off or to make clear how valuable was his time.

Rory Gifford, in contrast to the peacock Bliss, had the slightly dishevelled air of having just climbed from his bed and flung on whatever was nearest to hand. But the careless bohemian look suited him. It went well with his gipsy-dark good looks and curly hair. It gave him a devil-may-care appearance that was surely as contrived as Bliss's. They both worked in TV where image was all. It seemed probable that both men had thought long and hard about which image would best suit their purposes: the well-groomed, but friendly and chatty doctor to whom one could tell anything and the rakish, but intense and driven producer whose generally tense posture was meant to be indicative of the creative forces within. Or so Rafferty supposed. Such deliberate image-manipulation always inclined him to wonder what might lie concealed beneath.

As instructed, Llewellyn opened the interviews. Nothing new was revealed till Llewellyn asked if they now recalled seeing Jenny leave the first party.

'Surely, we don't have to go over all that again?' Gifford complained. 'You've already asked me this once and—'

Lancelot Bliss broke in. 'You shouldn't complain about the police repeating questions, Rory. It makes you look as if you've got something to hide.' This brought a scowl from Gifford. 'Besides, I've been thinking and now I *do* remember. Strange I didn't recall before really, because we were talking about that estate agent fellow at the time – what was his name?'

'Nigel,' Rory Gifford supplied. So far, he had contributed little to the conversation. But he didn't get a chance to say anything further as Lancelot Bliss again broke in and took over.

'Nigel. That's right. I remember now. Though a less likely Nigel I've never before met. And that *accent.*' Lancelot sniggered.

Rafferty asked tersely, 'What was wrong with his accent?'

'Poor chap was trying to do posh,' Lancelot told him. 'Made a hopeless fist of it. I thought he'd choke himself trying to elevate his normal voice to something approaching the Queen's when she was a young woman. Remember how unnaturally high-pitched her voice was then?'

Tight-lipped, Rafferty nodded.

'Way too ambitious of him, of course. Ironic really, because all the real movers and shakers do estuary-speak now in an attempt to mimic the common herd. If he'd stuck with his normal voice we might have believed he was *one of us* doing estuary-speak for all he was worth. As it was...'

Suddenly more talkative, Rory Gifford put in, 'What can you expect? Chap's an estate agent. All sharp suit and sharp practice presumably. I'm surprised Caroline allowed him to sign up with the agency. I mean, I thought it was supposed to cater for the professional classes.'

Rafferty thought they were being a bit harsh on the accent. He felt he'd done pretty well considering how nervous he'd been. 'Anyway, you were saying why you noticed when Jenny left the party,' he prompted Bliss.

'Sorry. Yes. I rather fancied poor Jenny, which is why I was put out when I saw this Nigel, all borrowed suit and plebeian sweat, follow her out. That would have been around 10 p.m.' He looked shrewdly at Rafferty before he asked with a casual air, 'I suppose he's top of your suspect list?'

'Mr Blythe has been questioned, like everyone else at the party,' Rafferty agreed blandly, determined not to reveal that – as far as the official investigation was concerned, anyway – Nigel Blythe was no longer a suspect. If he did, it might take the doctor's sharp eyes and mind no more than a hop, skip and a jump to realise how closely 'Nigel's' features resembled Rafferty's.

'Can't say I'm surprised the man's in the frame for murder. Though I thought, by now, his name and picture would have been made public.'

'We have our routines to go through, sir,' Rafferty replied woodenly.

Bliss nodded, but his mind had already moved on. 'To think I troubled to make conversation with him when all the time he must have been selecting his victim. Doubt you'll need to look any further for your murderer, Inspector. Ralph Dryden was right. This Nigel had a very furtive air, didn't he, Roar?'

Rory Gifford nodded.

It sounded as if the three men had been comparing notes. Not that Rafferty could blame them. As he knew to his cost, even the innocent found involvement in a murder enquiry an unpleasant experience.

'What about the night of the second party, sir?' Llewellyn broke in. 'Have you had any further thoughts on that which were not in your original statement?'

'Yes.' Bliss finished his coffee and dumped the mug on the table. 'I didn't mention that this Nigel chap turned up in the same suit. Same shirt, too, would you believe? Probably couldn't get his better-off friend to lend him another after he'd sweated so heavily into it the previous night. No wonder he was perspiring so freely when you think what he was planning to do. It's clear, now I've had time to think about it, that he picked out his second victim early on. Not only did he monopolise Estelle Meredith all evening, he went off into the night with her the same as he did with Jenny Warburton.' He gave Rafferty another shrewd look and added, 'Yet you haven't arrested him. I can't help but wonder why?'

Rafferty let him wonder. He breathed a sigh of relief a few minutes later when they left Bliss and Gifford to indulge their speculations. They seemed eager to thrust any guilt on to 'Nigel's' hapless shoulders. No doubt it would suit both men nicely. Just as well he had managed to suppress the fact that Nigel no longer had alibis for either night, though it worried him that Bliss, for one, had clearly been surprised that Nigel was still free. He could only hope the doctor's curiosity didn't prompt him to go to the super. Bradley tended to be a bit starry-eyed about media types and would be likely to trip over in his rush to check and reassure them that Nigel's alibis were kosher.

'I'm beginning to feel rather sorry for Nigel Blythe's imposter,' Llewellyn commented as they climbed in the car for their next appointment. 'It sounded as if he was completely out of his depth. If, as the facts indicate, he joined the Made In Heaven crowd with murder in mind, you'd think he'd want to blend in rather than stand out and attract attention. I wonder what could possibly have prompted him to join such an obviously unsuitable agency.'

It was handy, Rafferty silently answered. He also felt sorry for 'Nigel', though that was hardly surprising. 'Poor bloke's been judged and found guilty just cos he can't do "posh",' he agreed.

'To be fair, it wasn't just because of that,' Llewellyn was quick to remind him. 'There are plenty of witnesses to say that the man masquerading as Nigel Blythe was the person last seen with both victims. It's fortunate for the real Blythe that he's been exonerated.'

'Isn't it?' Rafferty replied, as, out of Llewellyn's sight, he crossed his fingers and wished it were true.

'I still think it's suspicious that he should be burgled just before the murders and that he should then be so conveniently supplied with alibis. You didn't think there was anything suspicious about those alibis?'

'No. Not at all,' Rafferty said hastily. 'The two women who supplied them struck me as honest, reliable witnesses.' His crossed fingers tightened as he ventured boldly on with a slanted truth. 'In fact, both of them said they had considered retracting their statements to protect their respective marriages from fallout. Understandable, I suppose, when you consider the potential embarrassment of having to stand up in a law court and admit to spending considerable time alone with Nigel in his bedroom' – even if one of them had been simply admiring his website, as Kylie Smith had originally claimed.

'I suppose so. It's just the coincidence that

bothers me. I know how little you like coincidences.'

'I'm happy enough with them when coincidences are all they are,' Rafferty assured him. 'No, the real Blythe's out of it. Accept it.' *Please* accept it, Rafferty silently pleaded. Thankfully, Llewellyn said nothing further on the subject.

Toby Rufford-Lyle, their next appointment, was another of the party guests who lived in some style: a detached house at the leafy end of East Street, which, with the spring sunshine lighting all the greenery, looked incredibly lush.

Rafferty took in the large, double bay windows and the imposing front door made of solid oak as Llewellyn turned into the generous, circular, shrub-lined drive. A sports car in British racing green was visible through the open door of the separate double garage.

Rafferty watched as Llewellyn the car buff indulged a brief, slack-jawed drool. Then duty reasserted itself and he joined Rafferty at the front door.

As Rafferty pressed the buzzer and waited for it to be answered, he mused wistfully on the enviable incomes and lifestyles of his fellow Made In Heaven members, especially the men. Lancelot Bliss, apart from his lucrative TV deal, also had a successful private medical practice. Rory Gifford, he knew, had made a name for himself by making use of his friend's medical knowledge, gift for informative witty one-liners and innate showmanship. And as for Toby Rufford-Lyle – *were* there any poor barristers, apart from the fictional Rumpole? He had certainly never met any.

If these were the people whose homes Nigel ran his tape measure over every day it was no wonder he'd sneered so at Rafferty's little flat.

When no one appeared in answer to his ring, impatiently, Rafferty pressed the buzzer again. It was strange such men couldn't find steady girlfriends. But, Rafferty answered his own unspoken question, perhaps that was the trouble. They could find any number of girlfriends keen to go steady with them; women would be likely to throw themselves at the Toby, Rory and Lancelots of this world. Presumably, that was the reason they had joined the agency. There, they had been assured, they would meet women of their own standing who wouldn't throw themselves at them. Or rather, who might still throw themselves at them, but who would do the throwing for reasons other than money. Ironic that in Isobel, the agency's secretary/receptionist, they had found a world-class gold-digger. No wonder there had been several complaints about her.

Of the main male suspects only Ralph

Dryden's wealth was spurious; worse than spurious. As Llewellyn's enquiries had revealed, Dryden had financially over-extended himself. For all the upmarket attractions of the warehouse apartments, they weren't selling quickly enough to resolve some severe cash-flow problems. It seemed that Dryden's myriad business interests were a house of cards – all interdependent. Thus far, Dryden's confident exterior had propped up the edifice. But the merest breath of doubt blowing against the walls of the card house risked the collapse of all. Had Dryden feared the precariousness of his business finances was about to be revealed, making a crash inevitable? If Isobel—

Rafferty's thoughts came to an abrupt end as Toby Rufford-Lyle appeared round the side of the house, his thick fair hair tousled and showing an engaging tendency to curl where it met his sweat-flecked neck.

'Sorry. I was in the garden,' he said. 'I like to try to keep the weeds down in case my gardener abandons me to the jungle and decides to retire.'

Toby's figure, though slim and remarkably boyish for his thirty summers, was lithe and tautly muscled beneath his brief shorts and T-shirt. Rafferty wondered if he worked out.

'Come round,' Toby invited. 'It's a warm day and I'm sure you'd like a cold drink.'

As they sat on the terrace at the back of the

house, appreciatively sipping what Rufford-Lyle told them were mint juleps, Rafferty let his gaze sweep over the extensive garden. *Jungle* looked about right, he thought. Although the terrace held myriad containers filled with sweet-scented English and French lavender, pinks and more exotic blooms Rafferty was unable to put a name to, the garden proper was so filled with tall trees and shrubs that it was completely secluded. Here, with the birds singing all around, it would be easy to imagine oneself in the depths of the country rather than in a suburban street.

Rafferty turned back to their host just as Llewellyn opened with his 'So tell me, Mr Rufford-Lyle—'

'Oh, call me *Toby*, please. I have to contend with so much formal "Mr Rufford-Lyleing" in my work that in my leisure time I like to drop it.'

Rafferty was surprised that Toby R-L should consider answering police questions during a murder enquiry akin to a leisure activity. But then he did work in a Chambers that specialised in criminal law, so must occasionally socialise with policemen. But whether he did or not, Rafferty was sure Llewellyn wouldn't become numbered amongst them; he hadn't even touched his mint julep, so could be relied upon not to take such a light approach. And so it proved.

'I prefer to keep to formalities, sir,' Llewellyn told him firmly. 'I've found it's better that way.'

Toby shrugged off his failed attempt to establish a 'legal brotherhood' and leaned back on his wooden garden bench to gaze briefly at the blue sky. He came back to earth to ask, 'Are you any nearer catching the chap who did these killings?' His boyish face, which must be an asset in a courtroom, broke into a strained smile as he added, 'Only my Head of Chambers has somehow got wind that I was there and it's making things really awkward for me. I'm between briefs just now and normally the clerk would have another waiting, but this time ... Well, as you see, I'm enjoying the unaccustomed luxury of free time during the working week. As a barrister it's expected that I only get involved in crime from the right side of the dock. Word's got round and the female staff are starting to avoid me.' His youthful jawline with its suggestion of golden down, clenched. 'It's becoming pretty unpleasant.'

'I'm sure,' said a not-unsympathetic-sounding Llewellyn. 'But it's only by conducting interviews like this one that we'll catch the person concerned.'

'Quite. Quite. I do understand.' After glancing briefly at the still silent Rafferty, he invited, 'Fire away then, Sergeant.'

Llewellyn took him through the questions

their earlier interviewees had been asked, but got little of any value in return.

'I wish I could be more help,' Toby apologised as he poured himself another refreshing glass from the jug on the table and told Rafferty – who needed no second invitation – to help himself to a refill. 'I'm usually very observant. I have to be in my line of work. I suppose it's because neither of the victims seemed my type. And then people were milling about all night from the drawing room to the cloakrooms and out on to the terrace. It was difficult to keep track. Of course, one didn't realise one would be a before-the-fact witness to murder.'

'I understand that, sir. But if anything further should occur to you.'

'Of course. I'd be only too happy if it did, Sergeant. The sooner these murders are cleared up the better I'll like it.'

They left Toby Rufford-Lyle sitting on his sun-dappled terrace under the pleasantly shading umbrella and made their way round to the car, which, by now, resembled an enclosed tropical greenhouse. They wound down the windows and headed back for the station, with Rafferty – who disliked hot weather as much as the Highlands-raised Sam Dally – for the first part of the journey at least, imploring his determinedly law-abiding sergeant to relent and put his foot down for once so they could get a rush of cooling breeze.

He subsided into sweaty silence as they crossed the river at East Street's western edge. Here the waters of the Tiffey made a lazy curl towards the outskirts of Elmhurst before straightening for the stretch down to Tiffey Meadow and beyond, as if it had finally smelled the sea and was intent on wasting no more time in leisurely meanderings.

Rafferty took the opposite course. Denied a refreshing stiff breeze, he retreated inwardly from the heat and speculated to himself about the case. Isobel's insistence that Estelle Meredith had been on their books for some weeks had been supported by the statements of the rest of the agency workforce, as well as by the computer. So why had Estelle lied to him? Was it only because she hadn't wanted him to think her used goods because she had been through the list and was now starting at the top with the new members?

Unless she had some kind of secret agenda, it was the most plausible explanation. But even if Estelle had had a secret agenda, Rafferty couldn't begin to guess what it might be.

And then there was Jenny Warburton. Jenny herself had said the party at the Cranstons' home had been her first, so, even though they continued to deny she was a member, who – but the agency staff – would know she would be there? Rafferty was about to blurt this out to Llewellyn and he just stopped himself in time, because, of course, this was another piece of 'Nigel'-knowledge. It hadn't been confirmed by the agency staff, nor could it be till this wretched part-timer deigned to return from her travels. Jenny's name hadn't even been entered in the appointments diary as his 'Nigel' had been, though this could be explained by Isobel's inefficiency. Of course, Jenny herself had confirmed the party was her first, which brought him back to square one...

This two-identity business was giving him serious problems. It was unfortunate that he had always had a tendency to open his mouth before engaging his brain. Several times he'd started to say something only to remember that he was talking – and remembering, as 'Nigel' – about something Rafferty the policeman could not possibly know. It was giving him another headache to add to the throbbing physical one.

He was rapidly approaching the stage where he wouldn't dare open his mouth at all in case he let something incriminating slip. But his unnatural reticence had brought its own problem. Several times, especially earlier in the investigation, he'd caught Llewellyn taking furtive glances at him as if he thought he was behaving oddly.

He was, of course. That was the trouble. And he'd have to continue to do so if his tongue wasn't to land him with even more problems. So, now he sat in the passenger seat, lips tight-pursed against any more unwise outpourings, and returned to his silent speculation. Where was he? Ah yes, at the fact of the agency staff being the only ones aware Jenny was likely to attend the party. It made every one of them prime suspects, even though they had all denied signing her up at all, which was pretty suspicious in itself. But at least the holidaying part-timer would soon be back; hopefully, she would clear up that particular discrepancy.

Of course, it was still possible that Jenny's and Estelle's murders had both been purely random killings. Rafferty had proved that anyone could join and attend parties before any criminal record could be checked out. As long as they provided a reasonably matching photo-ID document, which they could beg, steal or borrow as Rafferty had done. After all, he reminded himself, the murders had both been committed during dating agency parties where any psychopath could be certain of finding many young women looking for love. For such a creature it would have been a feast, a veritable banquet of opportunity. Any one of the female members would have been easy meat for a determined psychopath. Such a creature would believe the situation made for him and his base desires. And if these murders were premeditated, the killer would have taken appropriate precautions to avoid staining his clothes with the girls' blood. He could have easily left protective gear conveniently to hand in his car in New Hall's car park or amongst the shrubs in the grounds of The Elmhurst's annexe during a previous visit so it was to hand, and put it on before he indulged his passion for slashing.

Jenny could have just happened to be the unlucky victim – the first to leave and to leave alone and vulnerable and walk to the sheltered side car park. Anyone at the party could have seen Jenny about to leave alone and hurried out via the terrace to waylay her, thereby missing Rafferty make his way after Jenny via the drawing-room door. The same scenario applied to Estelle's murder also. Anyone could have noticed Rafferty depart, leaving Estelle alone on the bench in the annexe grounds.

Such a sadist could have joined the agency with the specific intention of finding vulnerable and lonely young women to kill. A dating agency could be the perfect setting for a psychopath to indulge his desires. Their strengths in appearing normal, indeed often described as 'charming', would help them to disarm their chosen victims.

A roomful of women looking for love and possibly with their guard lowered, believing that the agency had diligently checked out their members, would be a perfect habitat for a psychopath looking for a ready supply of victims. Dating agencies were first and foremost businesses run for profit. They couldn't afford to wait the weeks and months required for checking out a new signing's bona fides or criminal record. And they didn't. Rafferty had checked out half a dozen of the most prominent nationwide dating agencies and none of them went in for such checks so it was unlikely a small independent one would do so.

The thought that the murderer was still free to kill again spurred them on and, after a hurried lunch in the police canteen, they headed back out for the first of the afternoon interviews – with Caroline Durward and Guy Cranston, the two major partners in the agency.

Rafferty was determined they were going to release the names of *all* their members, past and present, whether they liked it or not. According to Llewellyn, Caroline Durward had complained bitterly about the damage already done to the business. But not, as he had been obliged to remind her via Llewellyn, as much damage as *not* catching the killer would cause.

Her protests had caved in after that. But

there was still some doubt whether they had been provided with *every* member's details. The agency was as upmarket as its literature had claimed. No doubt there would be several extremely important clients whom a protective Caroline had treated with such discretion that they hadn't even been entered in the agency's computer.

Rafferty's head and neck ached with tension. How could it be otherwise when they were now on their way to interview the woman who had more chance than most of recognising 'Nigel' behind the hairy mask and glasses. During the half hour he had sat across a desk from her, Caroline Cranston, née Durward, had had time in plenty to study him closely. Which was why, once past the congestion at the centre of town, what should have been a pleasant trip via country lanes lined with cow parsley and creeping purple saxifrage, through the small cottage-clustered hamlets of Elmwood and St Botolphe, turned into the trip from hell, with another all-too-real nightmare possibly looming at the end of it.

Twelve

The Cranston's home, New Hall, brought back all too poignant memories for Rafferty. And as he stretched his foot over the step where he and Jenny had lingered, he was again savaged by guilt so acute it was like a physical pain. He hurried down the hall after Guy Cranston as if he hoped to escape it, but the pain followed him.

Before they had reached New Hall the unpredictable April weather had suddenly turned from summer to winter. This had prompted the closing of the panelled dividing doors and the lighting of the fire, warmly shuttering the Cranstons in one end of the drawing room. The windows giving on to the terrace were also shut tight.

As was Caroline; Rafferty supposed she had a perfect right to feel aggrieved that her fledgling business could, like Jenny and Estelle, yet become another victim. Fortunately, though she had already vented most of her feelings on Llewellyn, Rafferty was conscious of emotions simmering beneath the outward politeness. Inevitably, this made for a tense atmosphere, which Guy Cranston seemed to feel it his duty to relieve. He wasn't noticeably successful.

After Llewellyn had gone through another round of introductions and routine questions, Rafferty decided to abandon caution and ask the question to which, as Rafferty, he knew only the *official* answer. 'Tell me,' he said as he lowered himself to the faded sofa, 'do you vet your clients with the Criminal Records Bureau?'

During his 'Nigel Blythe' interview he had agreed to the agency making the check. But this didn't mean they actually bothered to do so. There was still a backlog on these checks and those hoping to work with children took priority.

'We insist on background checks for all our members,' Caroline told him in a firm voice that didn't invite argument. 'Even though we cater for the educated, professional classes, we still need to be able to reassure the less self-assertive female members that they're not going to meet a predatory male.'

'These checks can take some time, I know,' said Rafferty. His comment immediately put Caroline on the defensive.

'Too long. It's extremely inconvenient. But we must protect our members. That has to be our priority.'

Rafferty caught Llewellyn's glance and although the Welshman didn't utter a word,

Rafferty could almost hear him say, *'The lady doth protest too much, methinks.'*

For the moment, he didn't push it, but as Nigel, he had been able to attend a 'Getting-to-Know-You' party and had been free to make dates and take telephone numbers as he chose, well before any answers to checks could have been received. It was interesting that Caroline had skirted round the truth. Was she merely protecting what remained of her business and the agency's reputation after the damaging press coverage? Or was she worried that she *had* let a predatory male loose? Maybe more than one...

Caroline became more defensive as the interview progressed as if the latter was indeed what she feared. She veiled her deceit with excuses. 'You must appreciate I have a business to run. At least I did, before—' She faltered for a moment and leaned towards the fire as if suddenly needing its heat to warm away the fear that her business might never recover from the double blow it had received.

Although Rafferty sympathised, it wasn't as if she would be destitute should her business collapse. She had a wealthy husband who was well able to support her. And although Caroline might not have checked her members out, Rafferty *had*. They had failed to find any convicted violent criminals, though that might be because, if there *were* such criminals among the agency's members, like Rafferty they had signed up under names other than their own. But at least the suspects still in the running, although not Persil-white, were mostly without a significant stain on their characters if minor drug busts and occasional drunken violence were discounted. Ralph Dryden had sailed stormy pecuniary waters several times, but always managed to reach the safe harbour of financial probity, though not without the Fraud Squad investigating his business methods. And Lance Bliss, like any successful doctor dealing with rich or neurotic females, had had several complaints of sexual malpractice lodged against him, none of which had held up.

Rory Gifford, though, was more interesting. He seemed to prefer diving in murkier streams. Though he was now the owner of a successful independent production company he had delved deeply in more seamy waters a few years earlier and still liked to make violent porn videos which dealt in images as violent as those captured by the police photographer. The moody, deep, bohemian image he cultivated wasn't merely a thing of surface show; he was deep and dark underneath as well. It made Rafferty wonder whether his taciturn behaviour had been for a very good reason, the very best reason of all: he had something to hide.

As if aware she had betrayed some culpability earlier, Caroline straightened and went back to defending her position. 'Potential clients won't wait for weeks for us to receive an answer as to their suitability. Besides,' she told them, 'we always warn our members to take sensible precautions. One of the reasons we hold our "Getting-to-Know-You" parties mostly in our own home is so we can watch over our newer members.'

Although Rafferty didn't remind her that such 'watching over' had done little to protect Jenny or Estelle, Caroline caught herself up and glanced at Guy as if seeking his support.

Guy supplied it readily enough. 'Caroline's right, Inspector. We really do as much as we can to protect our members. Our parties are always held in an enclosed setting, either here or somewhere with good security, like the annexe at The Elmhurst. I don't know what more we can do. We even give new members a list of sensible rules to follow.'

This was certainly the truth, as Rafferty's 'Nigel' had received a set of rules along with the map and invitations.

'But as my wife said, our members are all adults, successful, capable adults at that, rather than gullible teenagers. Educated professionals can be expected to have the sense to safeguard themselves, don't you think?'

Again, Rafferty forbore from the reminder

that Jenny and Estelle had both failed in this regard. Instead, he pointed out, 'But even educated professionals can be vulnerable through loneliness.' And as Rafferty reminded himself, even though he was a trained copper his state of mind had enabled the killer to make of him yet *another* victim. 'For committed psychopaths, there *is* no protection you can put in place that is going to be one hundred per cent effective. These people will always find their victims. That's the reason I requested access to *all* your members' details.'

He had put a faint stress on the *all*, but if Caroline had kept some details back she didn't betray herself. Instead, surprisingly, she looked a little mollified as if she thought his admission that no protection could be totally effective had given her a get-out clause.

Having abandoned caution, Rafferty decided he might as well pose another question. 'Who decided the cars should be parked to the side of the house rather than in front of it?'

Caroline shrugged. 'Oh, that's down to Guy, isn't it, darling?'

Guy broke in with a smile of rueful charm. 'I'm no doubt guilty of the deadly sin of pride, but I love this house, and when Caroline asked if some of the parties might be held here I insisted the guests park to the side. My wife may not love this house as I do, but I've always considered the front of the house imposing and dislike an array of cars breaking it up. Once through the hedge and parked up, they can't be seen from the drive.'

Convenient for the murderer, thought Rafferty. He would know exactly where to find Jenny when she went to drive home.

'Our friends are expected to obey the rule, too.' Caroline gave a tinkling laugh. 'Of course, they all know Guy's little idiosyncrasy.'

Her laugh made her seem less like Miss Robson, Rafferty's severe old religious teacher, and made her rather plain face almost pretty. For the first time, he was able to understand what the urbane Guy Cranston had seen in her. Rafferty asked, 'Is it only "Getting-to-Know-You" parties that are held here?'

'No,' Caroline told him. 'We hold more intimate parties also for our long-standing members, many of whom have become friends. Though some, like most of our newer members, are sensitive about the fact they make use of our services and don't want it becoming widely known.'

Rafferty nodded again. It was a sensitivity he shared. Anxiety that his shame would be discovered had been another reason to sign up under a name other than his own. The world at large – and Rafferty himself, he admitted – felt that only the sad and desperate signed up with dating agencies. The wags at the station would never let him forget it if it got out.

'My sergeant phoned the manager of The Elmhurst after Mr Farnell told us there had been a mix-up about the venue of the first party and he confirmed the mix-up. I gather you and Mr Farnell were both late arriving at the first party?'

Caroline nodded. 'One of Isobel's muddles, I'm afraid. I was annoyed at the time, though I blame myself for not checking. It looks so unprofessional to arrive late. When I spoke to her about it afterwards Isobel made no attempt to apologise and continued to deny the error had been her fault.' Caroline sighed. 'If only such muddles were her only drawback, but the way she *dresses* at the parties is another problem and gives totally the wrong impression.' She turned to her husband. 'Really, Guy, I know you took her on as a favour to her mother, but I think Isobel's going to have to go.'

Guy replied blandly, 'If you think so, darling. I'll have a word with her.'

Guy seemed to capitulate all too easily. But when Rafferty remembered Lance Bliss's comments about Isobel's pursuit of Guy, it was less surprising; like many men, Guy seemed happy for his wife to ease him out of a difficult situation.

'It was only by chance that I didn't head off for The Elmhurst myself,' Guy told them. 'I would have done, but Miss Warburton arrived just before I set out, so saved me a needless trip into town. Though, as Caroline says, by now we should all be aware of Isobel's little foibles and take the trouble to check the venue as she has something of a track record in that area.'

'Still, it must have been awkward supplying drinks and so on for such a throng with no warning?'

'That's not a problem,' Guy said. 'We hold so many parties here that we're always well stocked. We buy the stuff by the vanload. I have a sub-office in Calais and drive there a lot for business. I'll park the van up, and get taxis to and from my various business meetings. Then I stock up with lots of lovely cheap booze at the hypermarket. We have three of those enormous American fridges in the garage absolutely full of the stuff. And as we only serve nibbles at these affairs it's simply a matter of opening packets and emptying them into bowls.'

Rafferty remembered thinking it a pity so much booze was supplied but only nibbles were provided to soak it up. But perhaps that was done intentionally to loosen-up shy, newer members? It had certainly worked a treat for him at the second party.

Caroline and Guy Cranston were amongst those whose alibis hadn't been substantiated by a third party. Rafferty questioned them about it.

Caroline told them she and her husband had been together at the relevant times, having retreated to their study at the first party and to the room they kept on a permanent booking at The Elmhurst's annexe during the second.

'With Guy away so frequently I'm forced to snatch opportunities to update him on agency business. It never takes much more than half an hour, but for obvious reasons, when the updating occurs during party nights we have to wait till the party's got going as we can hardly be seen to abandon our clients to look after themselves early in the proceedings. You'd be surprised how much encouragement some of them need, for all they're meant to be confident professionals.' She frowned. 'But you already know all this.'

As if sensing that Caroline might be about to lose her temper at being forced to repeat herself, Guy volunteered some information. 'I spend so much of my time away on business that when I am here I prefer to be able to stay home. That's one reason why I agreed to the agency parties being held here.'

Guy smiled briefly. It was a smile of

singular charm and Rafferty found himself warming to the man.

Caroline said, 'Guy hasn't time to take much part in the day-to-day running of the agency. He's more of a sleeping partner, so it's good of him to allow his home to be invaded by the agency members when our evenings together are so precious. In fact, it was our wedding anniversary the night of The Elmhurst party. I baked a cake.'

Rafferty remembered it. The cake had been sliced and handed round with some ceremony, like a talisman to marital love. It had been good PR. Shame the cake had been too rich for his taste, though it had provided a much-needed lining to his stomach.

'I'm a lucky man, Inspector.' Guy put his arm round Caroline and smiled down at her. 'Most wives expect to be taken out on their anniversary; but not Caro. She knows how many evenings I have to eat restaurant or hotel meals while entertaining clients so a home-baked cake is a rare treat, even if it *does* have to be eaten at the annexe of yet another expensive hotel,' he added with a laugh.

'I have so few opportunities to spoil my husband,' Caroline confided, 'so it's a rare privilege when I'm able to.'

After learning of the semi-detached nature of their marriage Rafferty didn't doubt it. In spite or perhaps because of his lovelorn state, Rafferty found this marital mutual appreciation society no more to his taste than the anniversary cake. To conceal this, he asked Guy about his work.

'I'm an importer, Inspector, mostly from the Middle East, Africa, India: carpets, carved idols, all sorts of exotic merchandise. It's interesting work, but the travelling can be wearisome. Of course, I make use of agents in the countries I import from and the internet is a godsend, but I still like to check out new lines personally. It gives a good living, so I mustn't complain.'

'There's just one more question before we leave you in peace.' Rafferty rose. 'I understand that neither yourselves nor either of the full-time staff recall signing Jenny Warburton up as a member.'

'That's right,' Caroline told them. 'As I said to your sergeant, the computer entry was made by Emma Hartley, our part-time member of staff.'

'We can find no trace of Miss Warburton actually paying the joining fee. Have you any idea how that might have happened?'

Caroline said, 'Emma was in rather a bad mood on the day the computer shows Miss Warburton signing up. My fault, I'm afraid. It was Isobel's afternoon off and I'd asked Emma to work a little later than she normally would. She got in a bit of a temper about it. I imagine she overlooked the payment in her rush to get the paperwork done so she could go away on holiday.'

'I would like to see the relevant paperwork. I understand each new member has to fill out a form listing their personal details?'

'That's right. I imagine the original is locked in Emma's desk. I asked her son to hunt for his mother's office keys, but he was unable to find them. I suppose you could force it open, though it would be a pity as it was an expensive desk.'

'I doubt that will be necessary. I'll arrange for a locksmith to call in.' He paused. 'I understand this part-timer, Mrs Hartley, is not presently contactable?'

'I'm afraid not. She and her husband are touring the Continent, staying wherever the fancy takes them. I did try to get in touch with her, but when I rang her home her son said she had left in such a rush she forgot to take her mobile.'

'If you could let me have Mrs Hartley's home number,' Rafferty said, 'I'll speak to her son myself. Hopefully, he'll have some sort of itinerary for her, no matter how rough. I would like to speak to her as soon as possible.'

After Caroline searched in her briefcase, found her address book and gave them the details Rafferty made for the door. 'Oh and you will check that you've let us have all your members' details, won't you?'

This time, the faint suggestion that she might have been remiss about this made Caroline's lips thin. But her 'Of course' made him think he might have been wrong to suspect any such concealment. He thanked them and said, as he opened the drawing-room door, 'That's all for now.'

As Guy stood up to see them out, Rafferty recalled the cleaning lady who had cycled through the Cranstons' entrance gates as he arrived at the first party. If she regularly worked so late she must have encountered some of the party guests. By now, all too conscious that such a Nigel-knowledge question must be worded circumspectly, he said, 'This is a big house. Do you employ staff of any sort?'

'Only a cleaning lady. Annie – Annie Dobbs. Lives in the village. Last house on the left as you drive through St Botolphe,' Guy replied. 'My wife's here by herself most of the time, so it doesn't get really messy.'

'What about when you hold your party nights?' he asked.

'Certainly, it gets pretty messy then.' Guy laughed. 'You wouldn't think educated professionals would be such slobs. But they put wet glasses down on polished surfaces, slop red wine on the fabrics and cause no end of work.'

'Mrs Dobbs constantly complains about it,' Caroline put in from her seat by the fire.

'I sometimes think she loves this house more than Guy does.'

'Did Mrs Dobbs work here the day of the party as well as the day after?'

Caroline nodded. 'She works six days a week, Sundays too, when we've held a party on the Saturday. When that happens she takes the Monday off. I like to be sure the house is always ready for entertaining. My members are used to the best, Inspector. They would soon complain if they felt our standards slipped.'

Guy Cranston said nothing. But a little frown line had appeared between his eyes as if something had annoyed him.

Rafferty followed his line of vision and saw a glass lying under the hall table. It had contained red wine and the dregs had dripped out on to the carpet. It looked as if some tiny being had been done to death there.

After Guy saw them out, they walked round to the murder scene. The police tape had been removed. There was nothing to see but the industrial-size dustbins and the Cranstons' cars, and nothing but the gruesome pictures in Rafferty's head to indicate that this had been a scene of terrible violence.

They returned to the front of the building and climbed into their car, still parked where they'd reprehensively left it, in front of the façade that, in Rafferty's opinion, wasn't nearly as impressive as Guy Cranston thought. Strange how people could so easily delude themselves, Rafferty mused as they headed for the gates. 'We might as well see this cleaning woman while we're out this way.'

Llewellyn nodded. 'It's possible she may give us an insider's view on these agency parties.'

They already had that, though Llewellyn, of course, was unaware of it. He hoped this Annie Dobbs had seen or heard something which might give them a lead. They had precious few so far. And for all the good it had done for Rafferty to put himself through the risk of being recognised, he had learned little more than when he had sat back in the office devouring the reports as they came in.

Still, it was possible Mrs Dobbs might have picked up on whether Estelle, at least, had been involved with any of the other members. Jenny had told him she had been as new a member as Rafferty himself. Of course, it was always possible she had lied, like Estelle, though the computer entry made that less likely. But there had been a mix-up over her payment so it was possible there had been another mix-up also. Maybe this part-timer, Emma Hartley, who struck Rafferty as almost as inefficient as Isobel Goddard, might have concealed a backlog of new members for days before she got around to entering them on the computer.

Guy must have been listening for their car to start up because as they approached the gates they did an *open sesame* routine and Llewellyn nosed the car out on to the road and pointed it left.

Fortunately Mrs Dobbs was at home. She led them through to her kitchen and invited them to sit down. On the kitchen table was an array of brass ornaments that she had been in the middle of polishing. She picked up her rag and continued with her polishing. 'I wondered when you'd get around to seeing me.'

Here was yet another quibble. Rafferty sighed faintly and asked, 'Do you ever work late at New Hall, Mrs Dobbs?'

Annie Dobbs nodded, but didn't stop her energetic polishing. 'Pretty often. Usually before and after they have their agency parties.' For a brief moment, Annie Dobbs stopped polishing. She raised her head and her brown eyes settled worriedly on Rafferty. 'For all that I love the house, I'm not sure I want to continue working there now. It's not as if I was happy with some of the goings-on. And now, with these murders...'

'Goings-on?' Rafferty repeated. 'What sort of goings-on?' How many kinds were there? Rafferty asked himself. The only goings-on he could imagine Mrs Dobbs referring to would be those of a sexual nature. And so it proved.

'Most of their party guests tend to get a bit merry, but some of their more long-standing members take downright liberties. Give Caroline her due, she does try to put a stop to any promiscuity going on in the house, but she can't keep her eye on all of them all the time.'

'And which members would they be? Do you know their names?'

Mrs Dobbs was old-fashioned and it took a while to extract the details. Ralph Dryden, the property developer, was one. Another was Rory Gifford, the TV producer. Rafferty was surprised to learn that Dr Lancelot Bliss was yet another of those Mrs Dobbs named as 'taking liberties'. All had been guilty on different occasions of making for the bedrooms with several tipsy young women in tow.

'Mind you,' she added, 'they were only taking their cue from the host.'

'Guy Cranston? You mean he used to do the same?'

'Not when Caroline was there; he was the soul of discretion then. But when her back was turned ... God knows what he gets up to on his foreign trips. Caroline turns a blind eye. I remember she said to me once that Mr Cranston was a very *physical* man – said he needed an outlet.' Mrs Dobbs snorted and rubbed the current brass with even more vigour. 'If my Bert carried on like Mr Cranston and them others, I'd find him an outlet all right – I'd hand him a spade and tell him to double-dig the vegetable plot. Be fit for nothing after that.'

Mrs Dobbs's revelations tied in with what Lance Bliss had said – about the Cranstons having a semi-detached marriage and that Caroline gave Guy a long leash. Had he somehow managed to wrap this leash around his own neck?

The inquisitive Isobel could scarcely have been ignorant of such goings-on when they happened under her nose, especially as it seemed likely she formed part of them. If news of them had got out, Dr Lancelot Bliss, for one, might have been dangerously compromised. He might even have lost the lucrative TV job he clearly relished so much.

And then there was Caroline – Caroline with her romantically themed office and seemingly unromantic marriage. What did *she* think of its semi-detached nature? She was a Catholic, so Llewellyn had discovered. Rafferty thought back to some of the Catholic wives he had known in his childhood; stoics all, each had gained strength from their faith, strength enough to cope with their frequently wayward husbands. Did Caroline share that strength? According to the all-knowing, gossipy Lance Bliss, she cut the 'physical' Guy plenty of slack.

Lancelot Bliss had been more than generous in the gossipy information he had supplied about Isobel, Simon Farnell and Caroline and Guy Cranston. But he had become surprisingly reticent when asked about himself. Bliss appeared perfectly willing to gossip with a stranger about the agency partners and staff. What was it he'd said about Simon Farnell later on the evening of the first party?

'Simon, as I imagine you noticed, is a rather predatory homosexual. I sometimes think he only put up the money to make partner in the agency because he believed he'd find lots of "closet" type males would come within his orbit. I don't think he's been disappointed. But my, what a down he's got on little Isobel. I often wonder what she can have done to so incur his dislike. Caro, too, though that's more easily understood. Simon's got this yen to start a homosexual side to the dating agency. He's convinced it would be a big payer. Guy would be happy enough to give him the go-ahead as long as it didn't cost too much to get off the drawing board. It's Caro who's the stumbling block. She's a dyed-in-the-wool Catholic of course and takes the line that homosexuals are the Devil's spawn.'

Rafferty recalled he had asked the by then well-oiled Bliss, 'So how on earth did Farnell manage to persuade her to allow him to become a partner?'

Bliss had sniggered. 'By hiding his homosexual light under a bushel, of course. Our Simon can be quite the devious little queen when he sets his mind to it. He dressed and acted like a really hetero male. Flattered her, flirted with her, the usual stuff. Caroline's not the most adept at telling flattery from the real thing and Simon can be a determined flatterer when it suits him. Caroline adores Guy, but he saves his most outrageous flattery for the women he's trying to bed.'

'How on earth did those two ever get together?' Rafferty had asked. He found himself quoting Nigel. 'They don't seem much of a mirror-image.'

'Guy being so good-looking and Caro so plain, you mean?'

'Something like that.'

'His first wife died eight years ago. She was driving when the brakes apparently failed. There were the usual rumours, but nothing was ever proved.'

'Rumours? What do you mean?'

Bliss's shoulders shrugged in their beautifully cut jacket. 'His first wife had inherited this house and a pile of money a few months before her death. Guy came in for the lot. I never believed the rumours myself. Guy really loved his first wife. He was devastated when she died so suddenly. I often wonder whether he married Caroline on the rebound as he had barely known her a matter of months. But she was a great support when he needed a shoulder to lean on and they've made a go of it, though I suspect that's more down to Caroline than Guy. She loves him, so puts up with his straying. Though I rather think she drew the line at Isobel. Bit much when the straying includes one's staff, I suppose, even if the staff has blue blood running through its veins.'

His remembered conversation with Bliss reminded him of Isobel. Again, he wondered why Guy had told Lancelot Bliss about the dire financial position of Isobel and her parents. He must have known the gossipy Bliss would spread it around. It was an unkind thing to do, particularly after he had bedded the girl. Neither was it altogether ethical for a partner in the business – even a '*sleeping*' partner as Guy was, in more ways than one – to thrust a gold-digger into the midst of the agency's unsuspecting clientele, though Rafferty, remembering the mostly self-confident, occasionally arrogant profiles of his brother members, judged they would fend for themselves well enough.

It would be interesting to see if Isobel was finally given the sack; if not, it would be an indication that she did indeed know more about Guy and the rest than they would like. Knowledge was power, especially when you were as desperate as Isobel was said to be. And Cranston only had his wife's alibi to back him up for each murder.

There was another question mark against Guy Cranston. It seemed that he and Rafferty shared similar tastes in women. They had both fancied the same two girls and both girls had wound up dead. Coincidence? Or what?

As Llewellyn had remarked, Rafferty had never believed in coincidence, so it must be – or what. But *which* what, that was the question?

On his arrival at the first party, Guy and Jenny had been chatting perfectly amicably. But later, when he had returned with second drinks for himself and Jenny, the atmosphere between the two had seemed tense. She had been short with Guy, dismissive. Why? What could possibly have happened between them during the brief interval between Rafferty going for the drinks and his return? Had Guy taken the opportunity to make an approach to Jenny? Surely the man wouldn't be so indiscreet, especially when his wife had just arrived?

He would have liked to debate the point – that and many others – with Llewellyn. But he daren't. Rafferty knew himself well enough to be aware that, in his eagerness to score over the logical Welshman, restraint usually went out the window. So instead, after a detour to The Elmhurst to look at the scene of Estelle's murder, they headed for Ralph Dryden's office and the final interview of the day.

Thirteen

Dryden's office looked as if he had been squatting in it; a sleeping bag had been rolled up and stashed behind a cushion on the settee, but it was still clearly visible. The small filing room just off his office held what, behind its concealing curtain, looked like a rack of clothes. Were Dryden's finances in an even worse state than they'd thought for him to be reduced to camping out in his office?

As Rafferty studied Dryden, he thought they might be. The well-groomed property developer no longer looked quite so glossy and well-cared-for. He had a scab from a healed shaving cut on one of his chins and the professional manicure of his fingernails had a ragged, just-chewed look.

Although he was intelligent enough to give them a polite welcome there was a tight-wound air to him. It was clear Dryden was a man on the edge; his business empire tottering, his shaky finances made shakier by the possible depredations of a blackmailing Isobel.

Now he was also a suspect in a double murder enquiry. Any one of these things could be enough to send a man over that edge, but the three together might make a person dangerously unpredictable, especially if they *had* already killed and killed again. If she *was* blackmailing this man, it wasn't surprising Isobel had taken fright and returned to her parents' home in Suffolk. The wonder was that she had dared to return.

Rafferty glanced questioningly at Llewellyn, but all he received in return was a tiny shrug. Llewellyn had obviously not suspected how far advanced was Dryden's plight. Clearly, this was a very recent downturn.

Although it was not yet five in the evening, there had been no secretary in the outer office. Had he had to let his staff go as well as his house? Dryden seemed desperate to make light of things and reassure them as if they were worried shareholders instead of disinterested policemen. It was as if he feared that more than his financial security rested on their believing him.

'It's just a blip in the old cash-flow,' he said. 'Bit of strategic retrenching till the apartments sell. Nothing that more aggressive marketing won't put right.'

Rafferty suspected the reassurance was as much for Dryden as for them.

They didn't stay long. Just long enough to question him about Isobel. 'It's been implied that Isobel Goddard has another talent at her fingertips other than poor typing,' Rafferty began.

Dryden just stared at him, saying nothing, though his body hunched.

'Aren't you interested in knowing what that talent might be?'

Dryden shrugged. 'Not particularly.'

Rafferty decided to pretend to greater knowledge than he possessed. 'Of course you know Isobel well, don't you, sir? I imagine you're familiar with her usual methods of extracting money from the men in her life.'

That caused Dryden to sit up. He met Rafferty's gaze with all the practised innocence of someone who had successfully gone through the Fraud Squad's wringer on several occasions. 'I don't know what you mean, Inspector.'

'No? You're obviously one of the fortunate few then.'

It was clear that Ralph Dryden wasn't to be surprised into an admission. He was obviously too preoccupied with his own troubles to be pinned down on other matters, so after promising him they would return when he was in a state of mind more conducive to providing answers, they left and returned to the station where they wrote up their reports before Rafferty made his lonely way home.

* * *

That evening, as on so many nights, Rafferty sat alone in his flat. He was in a maudlin mood as he brooded over several nightcap glasses of Jameson's. How many others were, like himself, he wondered, sitting alone and lonely right now?

Was Ralph Dryden one of them? Strange to think he might be sharing the solitary midnight hour with the property developer.

Loneliness, as he had discovered, made people especially vulnerable; high-flying career women – and men – who had no one to go home to as well as pretty young women like Jenny and Estelle. Why else would they have joined a dating agency?

How many of them lacked friendly neighbours who took an interest or a close-knit family such as he had? Admittedly, his family as often caused him grief as gave him pleasure or support, but at least they were *there*.

Community was mostly a forgotten concept, he informed the television newscaster with a sweep of his arm that wastefully distributed whisky over the carpet. How many like him, he demanded of the Anglian newsreader, were forced to have one-sided conversations with the one-eyed and self-absorbed friend in the corner of the room? Solitary lives encouraged lonely people into dangerous waters where sharks – and worse – basked while they awaited their prey.

The dating of strangers was an everyday occurrence. Local papers, Sunday papers, internet sites, all had their columns of sad people striving to make themselves sound appealing; it was what had put him off going that route. Dating agencies provided a service from strangers to introduce strangers to other strangers. And some of these strangers were – as this Lonely Hearts case proved – very strange indeed...

Given such brooding melancholy, it wasn't surprising that when he finally stumbled his way to bed Rafferty had another nightmare, one of the worst yet. The pictures in his head had been so vivid, the battered and slashed bodies of the two victims so bloodily graphic, that, already worried about his fading memory of both party nights, he had begun to wonder if he *had* killed the two girls and was in a state of denial. As well as the headaches and nightmares from which he woke sweat-drenched and with the shakes, he'd been having the occasional blackout when he'd come to and found a mug of tea beside him that he couldn't remember making and food in the fridge that he couldn't remember buying. He wondered if he was going mad. Because worst of all, in his nightmares, the face of the killer was now his own.

He sat up and turned on the bedside light.

And as he stared into the room's corners where the light didn't reach, he worried again that it had been Nigel, his alter ego, who had been the last person to see both girls alive. The thought was preying on his mind more and more. The blackouts made him realise he could no longer remember where he had been around the time of the girls' murders – had *he* been the one to follow Jenny to the Cranstons' lonely car park and kill her? His previous recollection of saying goodbye to Estelle had vanished also. It was strange that he could remember, if vaguely, earlier episodes of both evenings yet now could no longer remember these crucial times. It was almost as if his mind was protecting him from knowledge he would rather not have.

He broke into a cold sweat as he asked himself, *could* I have killed them? Could that, rather than the high-minded, almost knightly desire to avenge the two victims, be the *real* reason why he was so protective of his secret and his cousin and was doing his damnedest to divert suspicion?

It was true what he had told Llewellyn; he *had* been getting a lot of headaches. He had put them down to wearing his father's spectacles, as the headaches hadn't started till he had begun to wear them. But he now wondered if the main cause of these headaches wasn't the bang on the head he had mentioned to Llewellyn. Funnily enough, he remembered telling Llewellyn that the bang on the head had happened before the murders, while Llewellyn was still on honeymoon. But was that true? Or was his previous conviction that this was so simply another example of his mind's subconsciously protective games? But whatever explanation was the right one, it was certain that now he could no longer recall precisely when it had happened.

Between his headaches and his increasingly wakeful nights, his recollection of so much was becoming confused. He would have made an appointment with his doctor if it hadn't been for the murders. Now, with the episodes of amnesia, he was scared what he might reveal during an examination.

He didn't know how much longer he could keep up the twin penances of this investigation and his own sorry deceptions. Sometimes, all the lies and evasions sickened him. Once or twice he'd felt on the verge of confessing all to Llewellyn. The only thing that stopped him was the belief, deep in his soul, that in spite of his doubts, his real fears and his nightmares, he was guilty of nothing worse than being an unlucky fool. It was only after he awoke from yet another nightmare that the doubts and fears began again and he recalled the insistence of psychologists that we were all capable of murder...

Suddenly, desperately afraid, anxious to drown out such thoughts, Rafferty threw back the bedcovers, crossed to the living room and turned the TV back on.

Against his better judgement and desire, he dropped off to sleep again, stretched out on the settee. But it was a blessedly dreamless sleep. He woke late, feeling dazed and sluggish. Somehow, he dragged himself in to work, accompanied by the thought that a few short weeks ago all he had to worry about – well, apart from his failure to get to grips with another murder case – was the suit Llewellyn intended to wear at his wedding. It seemed pretty small beer now.

But Rafferty, who always thought of himself as a pessimist with an optimist ever striving to break free, let the optimist have a fleeting glimpse of the open prison door with the reminder that he had got out of that problem okay in the end – before Superintendent Bradley arrived in his office like a man-o'-war in full battle array and proceeded to blast the optimist's trapdoor to freedom with salvos of fault-finding.

'You're expected to be an efficient manager of manpower, Rafferty,' he told him. 'It's our ultimate resource. Yet now I find you've been squandering it as if it cost nowt, on an endless round of unnecessarily repeated interviews. How many times does a so-called witness have to write a statement saying they saw bugger all before you're satisfied? It can't go on, I'll tell you now. I'm a Yorkshireman and believe in plain-speaking, as you know.'

Rafferty did know. He could take a fair guess at what came next, too. 'What will Regions say?' Rafferty muttered to himself seconds before Bradley.

'What will Regions say about such a waste of resources?' Bradley was visibly palpitating at the thought. 'I want some results, Rafferty. I don't want to be forced to ask for further funding when you've carelessly frittered away what you had; it reflects too badly on me – us. Just give me some results, man, that's all I ask. I know you pushed for us to go the DNA route on those party guests. But I don't want to do that unless I have to, it's bloody expensive. Anyway, it shouldn't be necessary if you were conducting the investigation in a competent manner. Detectives *detect*, Rafferty. At least they did in my young day. We didn't need all this newfangled assistance to help us find our man. Just do the job you're paid to do. You know I'll back you to the hilt and beyond if you do.'

And pigs might fly, thought Rafferty as the optimist within pulled his squashed fingers from the trapdoor and, with a quiet whimper, nursed their pulsating ache against his chest. But not a plain-speaking Yorkshire porker like you, he mouthed after the door-banging superintendent.

In search of sympathy, Rafferty went to the Lonely Hearts Incident Room.

He was aware he looked rough, his eyes bloodshot, the skin beneath them deeply marked with fatigue; the several curious glances his appearance attracted from the team were deeply worrying. Anxious that during each absence from the station something revealing might be discovered, each time he returned to work he felt a sense of foreboding as he waited for all hell to break loose.

Had something been discovered overnight or even before his late arrival? Had Smales shown another piece of untimely initiative? Had Kylie Smith, Kayleigh Jenkins, or both rung in to find out why he hadn't acted on their alibi retractions and arrested Nigel?

Nothing was said this time at least. But Rafferty noticed that even Llewellyn was giving him concerned looks. Was Llewellyn merely worried about his physical appearance? Or was he, too, beginning, like Rafferty himself, to suspect he might actually *be* the murderer made flesh?

Llewellyn was sharp. Though not given to listening to canteen gossip, he usually managed to keep abreast of who on the team was doing what and why. His altered appearance, his uncharacteristically devoted study of the paperwork and his previous – until Bradley had ordered otherwise – equally unusual reluctance to leave the confines of the station unless it was to venture far from the main witnesses, would be enough for Llewellyn's head to fill with questions. He had only to consider exactly *when* Rafferty had changed both his appearance and his behaviour and he couldn't help but make the connection.

The dangers of such a connection being made were increased when Bill Beard popped into the Incident Room to have a word with one of the team. Beard, who had been at the station longer than anyone in the room, considered himself something of an institution – a privileged institution – and rarely stood on ceremony. He certainly didn't when he placed himself foursquare in front of the board with the identikits of 'Nigel Blythe' pinned to it and observed, in front of the entire team, that the photofits looked a bit – no, quite a lot – like Rafferty.

If he was expecting some laddish response from Rafferty he was disappointed. For Rafferty was struck dumb as all the heads in the room swivelled, first to study the photofit and then to study Rafferty.

The worst of it was Rafferty knew he hadn't reacted naturally. At any other time, on any other case, he'd have made a joke about his many criminal forebears who had kept both the hangman and the crew of Australian-bound prison ships in full employment. But this time he'd just stood there not saying a word, with his easily read features doubtless proclaiming guilt from every pore.

Everyone in the Incident Room went strangely quiet after that. Rafferty, desperate to get away from eyes that, after studying him curiously, now seemed to his guilty conscience to be doing their best to avoid meeting his gaze, hurriedly handed over to Llewellyn and left the room.

In the solitude of a cubicle in the Gents' toilet, Rafferty convinced himself that several pairs of those eyes had looked at him as if they were reassessing his reason for his recently altered appearance. He had, when he had first adopted the disguise and confounded such intimates as his ma, Llewellyn and Maureen, congratulated himself on the success of his altered looks. Now it occurred to him that if Llewellyn or one of the smarter officers on the squad proved dogged enough to trace his family connection to Nigel, they might just look at him *and* his disguise and come up with the old two-plus-two answer.

And as he sat staring at the biro and knife-cut comments and jokes on the grimy walls, he admitted his own surprise that his deception hadn't been discovered long since. Surely, he thought, by now Llewellyn had mentioned the name of Nigel Blythe to Maureen and heard her astonished response? But if he had, Llewellyn had said nothing to Rafferty. The suspense, the strain of waiting to be found out, was getting to him. He was overcome with the desire to remain locked in his little hermit's cell in the Gents' till it all, somehow, went away.

But after half an hour's brooding solitude, Rafferty knew that wasn't going to happen. If it went away it would only be because he made it do so. But at least his lengthy lavatory-languish had given him some respite and time to engage in a game of 'What if?', which resulted in the tiniest oddity about the case forcing itself from subconscious hibernation into the half-light of his dim cubicle.

It had been the gossip loving Lancelot Bliss, he thought, who had made the comment that was currently tickling Rafferty's curiosity. It might be nothing, of course. Probably was. Even so, it was the first lead he'd had. Maybe Bliss would be able to enlighten him further. He seemed to know everything else about all those with a connection to the dating agency.

Rafferty felt a shiver run through his body and knew it was the first stirrings of hope. He hurriedly left the toilet and made his way to his office where he flicked through the list of the party attendees and found Lance Bliss's phone number.

In the way of such things, that one oddity had reminded him of another. The two of them added up to one very interesting pointer to guilt. Mercifully, it wasn't pointing at him.

Fourteen

Unfortunately, Lancelot Bliss seemed to have become elusive. After trying the doctor's consulting rooms and learning it was one of his studio days, Rafferty obtained the studio number. But Bliss, busy recording his TV show, was unable to come to the phone. Rafferty left a message, but when, forty minutes later, Bliss still hadn't got back to him he rang the studio again only to learn that Bliss had left. Next he tried the doctor's mobile, but it was turned off. His medical secretary told him Bliss wasn't expected in at all.

And although he rang the mobile number repeatedly throughout the rest of the day, Bliss failed to respond. Surely, a doctor like Bliss would make certain he could be contacted at all times? So why was he so determinedly out of reach *now?*

After leaving messages at all the locations at which he thought Bliss might turn up, he put the man from his mind. He could do no more about him for the moment. He had left Llewellyn in charge of the Incident Room and now Rafferty decided to remain quietly in his office, hoping that, since his faulty memory had released one piece of information, others would follow.

But further pieces of information proved as elusive as Bliss. In the end, he decided to stop badgering his mind and wait for it to throw up facts when it was ready. By the end of the day he had read the latest reports in between ringing Bliss, who remained as untraceable as any other titbits of memory.

Rafferty remembered he was expected at his ma's that evening. He'd promised to do a bit of weeding and some late spring pruning. He considered putting her off, but perhaps some physical work would free up his reluctant brain. Besides, he knew, if he didn't go, he would only sit brooding at home into the early hours, allowing his hopes to rise that he might be on the way to solving the case – and all on the basis of a couple of scraps of remembered conversation which might turn out to be of no importance at all. And might even – given his shaky recall – not even be accurately remembered.

His ma looked him up and down when he arrived. 'Whatever have you been doing to yourself?' she asked. 'You look like something the cat dragged in.'

'I've not been sleeping well,' Rafferty admitted.

'It's this unsettled life you lead, Joseph, all this dashing off chasing murderers and interrogating practised liars can't be good for a person. A man needs some stability, some certainty in his day-to-day affairs. I don't suppose you've been eating properly either?'

Rafferty, who had hardly been eating at all, though he'd been drinking plenty, was about to deny this, anticipating she would use any such admission to arm her insistence that what he needed was a wife.

But to his surprise, she said nothing of the sort. Instead, she made him sit down by the fire and wouldn't hear of him tackling her garden until he'd had an hour's rest, a cup of tea and a sandwich. She didn't torment him with questions, either, but let him sit quietly while she got on with her knitting.

With all his troubles, Rafferty had almost forgotten Ma's first great-grandchild was due in a few months. But the rapidly growing little lemon cardigan dangling from his ma's knitting needles reminded him. It was a shock to realise that young Gemma's baby would make him a great-uncle and elevate him to the generation that was supposed to set an example, not turn into a signpost showing the way to Folly Road.

It gave him something else to think about during the two hours he spent on the garden, pruning, weeding and generally doing the heavy work that his ma was no longer able to manage.

An inquisitive blackbird flew down while he was working and stared at Rafferty from a distance of two feet, his head on one side as if to enquire what Rafferty was doing in *his* garden.

'I suppose you want me to find you some worms?' Rafferty asked it. The blackbird didn't deny it, so Rafferty dug his spade into the soil of the shrub border. He struck one of the slug baits his ma had dotted around the garden. Filled with beer, her baited jam-jar trap had worked a treat; it contained two bloated and very drunken slugs. He eased them out, whacked them with a spade and tossed them towards the blackbird, who bobbed his head as if in thanks, seized one of the fat slugs and flew off.

Half an hour later, Rafferty eased his aching muscles and stood back to admire his efforts. The garden looked good and he felt pleasantly tired after his exertions. He put the tools away, washed and returned to the living room, where he sat down and prepared to let his ma spoil him. Yes, he said, he was more than willing to stay for a bit of home-cooked supper. Anticipating his arrival, his ma had shopped for and cooked one of his favourite meals: steak and kidney pie with more vegetables than he could eat, with apple crumble and custard to follow. Although he had intended going home after the meal, instead, pleasantly full, he sat down and gave his digestive system a chance to work. And as he watched a film on TV with his ma, a curious thought sidled into his brain.

At first, he doubted the conclusion the thought brought him to, but when he put it together with the other scraps he had earlier recalled, the more it seemed to him that he might be on to something at last, something tangible.

Though the possibility excited him, it couldn't fight the heavy meal or the mental, physical and emotional tiredness and he dozed off. To his horror, when he woke from the midst of another nightmare, it was to find his ma staring at him.

'Whatever's wrong, Joseph? You were screaming out something that sounded like, "My God, the blood, the blood. What have I done?" ' She sat beside him on the sofa and asked plaintively, 'What *have* you done? I know something's badly wrong.'

Worn down between the twin horrors of his nightmares and his guilty conscience, his earlier hopes forgotten, Rafferty gave in to the increasingly urgent desire to confess. He had to unburden himself to someone and with her flexible attitude to the law and law-breakers his ma was the obvious candidate, even if, once she knew of his various follies, she'd give him even more hell than he was currently experiencing.

But once again she surprised him and heard him out in silence as he told her the whole story: about joining the dating agency using his cousin's identity; that his 'Nigel' was suspected of murdering the two girls; about the pretend burglary he'd set up with her unknowing connivance; and about all the pressures he had been under for days – from Nigel himself, from Superintendent Bradley, from the retraction of Kylie Smith's and Kayleigh Jenkins's alibis and Timothy Smales's initiative that had brought these about. But – even to Ma – he couldn't bring himself to confess the fear that his nightmares might turn out to be true.

She took every one of his confessions in her stride. And after asking why he had felt it necessary to pretend to be someone he wasn't and why being a Rafferty wasn't good enough for him, she became briskly practical.

'They can't prove you've been masquerading as Jerry?'

Rafferty shook his head. 'Not unless Jerry comes clean, which he's several times threatened to do.'

'Leave Jerry Kelly to me. I know one or two things about that young man that he wouldn't like to see the light of day. If anyone does happen to ask where you were on those two nights, you can say you were here, with me.'

Rafferty was doubtful. 'The police generally don't give much credence to alibis provided by mothers,' he said.

'Do they not? Sure and I'd like to see your superintendent call me a liar to my face.'

So would Rafferty.

'Besides,' she added, 'is it not up to them to *prove* you weren't with me? Innocent until proven otherwise, that's what you've always told me the law says. And I should know because you've blasted the ears off me often enough about it every time some fool of a judge lets a violent criminal evade justice. But if I'm not enough of an alibi, we can always ask one or more of your brothers or sisters. The more the merrier. We can say we were having a family get together.'

'Too complicated, Ma,' Rafferty said as he thought how easily such a claim could be disproved. 'Best to keep it simple.'

'Simple it is,' she agreed. 'So, tell me more about these nightmares.'

Rafferty was still reluctant to tell her what it was about the nightmares that terrified him the most. But, of course, she got it out of him in the end.

'And you brought all this trouble on yourself because you didn't want me to know your business?' She shook her head. 'Sure and hadn't you only to say, son. Surely you knew that?' Luckily, she didn't give him the chance to deny it.

'So these nightmares you're so worried about – I take it you've convinced yourself your dreams might be recreating the actual event?'

Rafferty nodded. 'I can't get these pictures out of my head, Ma. The nightmares have degenerated to such an extent that in them I'm now the murderer. I see my face, all covered in gore and with a mad light in my eyes. I wake up with the shakes. I've never suffered such dreams in my life.'

For the first time during his revelations his ma looked disconcerted. 'Far be it from me to add to your troubles, son,' she said, 'but yes, actually, you have. Surely you remember the nightmares you suffered when you were about ten? It was after you nearly killed your sister, Maggie. You must remember.'

Dumbfounded, Rafferty could only shake his head to both questions.

'It was years ago, as I said, when the six of you were kids. Unbeknownst to me, you'd all been playing a game of "stretch" on the patch of grass behind the flats where we used to live in London. Your sister swore you deliberately threw the knife at her head instead of at the ground as you were meant to. Luckily, you helped yourself to my old, blunt knives instead of my best ones or you might well have done more damage. As it was, the knife just bounced off her head. She was hardly scratched for all her screaming that you'd tried to kill her. I told her that was nonsense. As if you'd do such a thing.'

Was it nonsense? Rafferty asked himself? Or had Ma merely been reluctant to admit to herself that her blue-eyed boy might be capable of such an act? Strangely, he had no recollection of the event. It had vanished from his memory. Why? Was it another case of guilty conscience? Another bout of violence that he'd managed to successfully bury even from himself?

He knew he would have to ask his sister for her version of events on that long-ago day. But for the here and now, Rafferty knew, if he was ever to be truly convinced of his own innocence then he had to prove who *had* killed the two girls and do it very soon. For his own peace of mind, his own sanity, it was essential he find out the truth – whatever it might turn out to be. He couldn't carry on much longer, not knowing for sure. But at least now he had something to go on.

Much later, when his ma had unearthed the bottle of brandy he had given her for Mother's Day, and they had both had several glasses, she returned to his reasons for joining the dating agency.

'Do you think me so lacking in understanding of what it is to be lonely that you felt you needed to do such a thing in secret,

Joseph? The Lord knows, I've had lonely times enough in my life.'

Rafferty's head jerked in surprise; Ma lonely? Such an idea had never occurred to him. She had a more lively social life than he did – not that that was difficult – but between his sisters, brothers, the grandchildren and the neighbours, his mother could hardly be short of company.

'I'm not talking about now,' she told him. 'Though living alone is not something I ever thought I'd get used to. I'm talking about when I was younger. Sure and wasn't I widowed in my thirties with you six to bring up on my own?'

Rarely, too rarely, Rafferty shamefacedly realised, had he thought of his mother and how she'd been left at his feckless father's sudden death. As she said, she'd been a relatively young woman – younger than he was now. He couldn't imagine being left alone and broke with total responsibility for six kids and he found himself looking at his ma with new eyes.

'I confess I'm hurt that you didn't turn to me earlier. I am your mammy, son. Haven't I often tried my best to find you a good woman?'

'Perhaps that was the trouble, Ma,' he said with sudden honesty. 'Didn't you tell me *your* mother did the same to you? And you took against every man she tried to fix you up with. And then you married Da.'

His ma studied him for a moment from steady brown eyes. Slowly she nodded. 'That I did. Told her I'd please myself. And I did.'

Rafferty felt they were at last beginning to have a true empathy.

Then his ma spoilt it by saying, 'And wasn't I sorry after? I should have listened to *my* mother.'

The implication being – so should you. But he'd wronged her again, as her next words revealed.

'But as you keep telling me, Joseph, you're a man grown and not my little lad any more. So you must please yourself. Pray God you make a better job of it than your mammy managed.'

She let a few moments elapse while they both considered this thought, then she rose, slowly, as if every bone had started shrieking its age at her and said, 'Your old bed's made up. Stay. It'll be company for both of us to think we've a loved one sleeping close.'

Rafferty nodded. 'I'd like that, Ma. Will I make some cocoa?'

'Cocoa? It's not cocoa we're wanting, the pair of us, but more of the same.' She jerked her head towards the brandy bottle. 'Might help you to have a restful night's sleep. It's what you need, more than anything. I'll make us both a hot toddy and bring it up. Go and wash the sadness from your face.

And don't forget to clean your teeth,' she shouted after him as he went out the door.

For the first time in days, Rafferty managed a genuine laugh. 'I won't,' he shouted back. He realised that he felt better and more hopeful than he had since he'd taken his first steps on his particular road to Calvary that was the Lonely Hearts investigation. Maybe, just maybe, he wouldn't end up crucified like Jesus Christ.

Fifteen

Although, when Rafferty got to work the next morning and tried Lancelot Bliss again, it was to find he still hadn't returned – someone else had – Emma Hartley, the holidaying part-time staff member of the Made In Heaven dating agency. He hurried over to Hope Street, anticipating a firm answer to one thing at least – who had signed Jenny Warburton up to the agency.

His expectation was disappointed when Emma Hartley denied doing so. 'It was some days ago,' he said. 'It might have slipped your memory.'

'It might, if I'd ever done it in the first place,' she agreed crisply. 'Or if I had the kind of mind from which things slipped. But as neither applies, I'm afraid you must look elsewhere for your answer.'

'You did forget to bring your mobile on holiday with you.'

She immediately contradicted him. 'No, I didn't. I loathe the beastly thing and left it behind deliberately. I don't see why Caroline thinks I should be at her beck and call when

I'm on holiday. Neither does my husband.'

Rafferty left and returned to the station. He knew when he was beaten. Emma Hartley exuded efficiency. Her movements were brisk, her desk a veritable icon to tidiness. He found it easy to believe she had the sort of mind from which nothing slipped. But it meant the mystery of who had signed Jenny up remained. Although the screen software showed Jenny had been entered on the computer under Emma Hartley's password, the staff all knew each other's passwords so any one of them could have entered the details. But they all continued to deny doing so. By now, even without Lancelot Bliss's additional input, Rafferty suspected he knew why. But how did he prove it? He retreated to his thinking zone in the Gents' to ponder the question.

The toilet at the station had provided a refuge more than once during Rafferty's police career, which was why it struck him particularly hard when even that sanctuary proved insufficient to keep life's outrageous slings and arrows at bay.

From his seat in the end cubicle, he heard the voice of Smales and one of his cronies as they entered the toilet and discovered he wasn't alone in regarding the lavatory as a refuge from the world at large and impossible superior officers in particular. Above the gush of the urinals as Smales and his friend made use of the facilities, he heard Smales reveal Rafferty's odd behaviour over the two York alibis.

'When I went to see the inspector I expected him to call Nigel Blythe in for questioning. But he didn't. I couldn't understand it,' Smales trilled. 'So I rang the two women again and do you know what they told me? They said that Inspector Rafferty had put the fear of God into them to such an extent they were reluctant to ring up to find out what was happening. I was dumbfounded, as you can imagine.'

His friend made encouraging noises of sympathy.

'Anyway, I was so worried at the thought of Blythe being free to kill again that I knew I had to do something about it.'

'So what did you do?'

'I went to see Sergeant Llewellyn last night,' Smales confided *sotto voce*, 'and told him all about it.'

'And what did Llewellyn say?'

Before Rafferty could discover the answer, he heard the door to the corridor open and other voices and machine noises filtered in. The door slammed shut behind Smales, his friend and whatever response Smales was about to make. In his cubicle, Rafferty put his head in his hands and groaned.

He had hoped his little chat with Smales about the need to keep things confidential in order to protect a possibly innocent Nigel would have kept Smales's tongue still. But even though discretion and Timothy Smales were not close acquaintances, he'd managed pretty well till now, as nothing had filtered back to Rafferty. Not unreasonably, the young officer hadn't thought himself to be breaking any confidence when he told Llewellyn all about it.

Rafferty supposed such an action was inevitable. On its own, Smales's puzzlement as to why Nigel still hadn't been arrested would have encouraged him to seek enlightenment. Rafferty admitted *he* hadn't been the most approachable of senior officers for some days.

Even if his guilty secret hadn't been about to be exposed, Rafferty had known in his heart that, despite his ma's staunch determination to provide him with an alibi, once either Nigel or Timothy Smales started singing, her alibi wouldn't fool anyone. And sing Nigel would because it couldn't be long now before he discovered his alibis were non-starters.

Once questions were begun, Rafferty knew his hastily donned new look would be exposed to dissecting scrutiny with the inevitable outcome. But at least he could go to see Llewellyn and try to make *him* understand; maybe, brainbox as he was, he might come up with a way of pulling his nuts out of the fire; though Rafferty didn't think even Llewellyn's brains equal to the task.

In a way, he was relieved it was all over. He supposed what he really wanted was for Llewellyn to say he believed him when he said he wasn't a murderer. But even that was an unreasonable expectation. How could Llewellyn truly believe in his innocence when Rafferty still wasn't convinced of it himself? Especially as he had contacted his sister earlier and learned her version of that long-ago game of stretch.

'Kill me?' Maggie had said when asked about it. 'You bet your life you meant to kill me. We hated one another in those days, don't you remember? I'd done something on you, can't remember what now, and you swore to get me.' She laughed. 'Damn nearly did too. You were a murderous little bugger in those days.'

His sister might now laugh about the incident, but her words had chilled Rafferty to the bone. His ma had said that at the time it had been passed off as an accident. But had it been an accident, he wondered now, or had the 'accident' been truly murderous in intent and the dangerous game used as the means to an end? A *knife*, he repeated to himself as he returned to his office and sat at his desk with his head in his hands. A knife had been one of the weapons used in both murders.

When his ma had brought their nightcap up the previous evening after he had confided about waking with the shakes from his nightmares, she had suggested he lay off the booze. Concerned about him, she had confided that, near the end of his life, his father had suffered episodes of the DTs, during which he had seen things that weren't there. Perhaps, she suggested, he was following a similar path to his father.

But, Rafferty thought, people had the DTs when they were awake. His delusions, if delusions they were, occurred when he was asleep.

But he knew he couldn't sit nursing his fears any longer. It was past time he confronted some of them. He had made up his mind to go to see Llewellyn privately. He had come to think of Llewellyn as being a good man to have at your side in a crisis. And if Llewellyn could somehow be made to believe him he wouldn't feel quite so bad about all the rest. This was as far as his reasoning had reached – if such a straw-clutching exercise could be termed *reasoning*.

Though Rafferty had resolved to confess all to Llewellyn, he didn't want to confess with Maureen present. So after going through the motions of working to get through the rest of the day, that evening he sat in the car and waited till he saw her come out of their flat and disappear up the road. But even then he didn't move. He wasn't relishing confessing to Llewellyn, with or without Maureen present. Only he was aware he couldn't carry on as he was, so he dragged himself from the car and made for Llewellyn's front door.

As he made his slow way up the path and raised his finger to the bell, Rafferty reminded himself that Llewellyn had mellowed since his marriage. But had he mellowed sufficiently to lessen the stiff-necked insistence that *all* law-breakers – whoever they might be – should face the full rigours of the criminal justice system? He guessed he was about to find out.

After Rafferty had confessed, he sat, hardly daring to breathe, while he waited for Llewellyn to speak.

But for once Llewellyn seemed to have nothing to say. Instead, he developed a serious case of the fidgets. He rose from his seat, walked to the opposite wall and began to fiddle with one of the pictures, a dreary portrait of a middle-aged man coloured in dull shades who looked almost as worried as Rafferty. Just to break the silence, Rafferty asked him what it was.

'It's a print of one of Rembrandt's later self-portraits.'

Rafferty nodded. Secretly, he thought the

painter would have been better advised to supply posterity with just the younger version of his face, but he wasn't really interested in Llewellyn's dreary picture selection. Tense from waiting for Llewellyn's reaction to his confession, he said, 'Never mind the bloody picture, Dafyd. Let the bugger stay bockedy. Come and sit down and talk to me. I didn't put myself through the torment of confessing just for you to ignore me. With all your fancy education you've surely got some advice as to what's best for me to do?'

Pleased when Llewellyn abandoned his picture-straightening and sat down again, Rafferty was less pleased when his sergeant quietly observed, 'I imagine you already know what you should do. You don't need my advice. You joined the dating agency under false pretences, using a false identity and with borrowed documentation. An agency, moreover, which had two of its members murdered shortly after you were seen with them. I don't think you have any choice but to go and see Superintendent Bradley, do you?'

Although he hadn't really expected any other response, Rafferty felt unaccountably disappointed. 'Be fair, Daff,' he said. 'I admit I did all that you say, but I did it in all innocence. You know what Ma can be like. Can you blame me for trying to keep from her the fact that I joined a dating agency?'

Somehow, he forced out the next words. 'It's not as if I murdered those girls. So help me out, man. How the hell do I prove I didn't kill them?'

Llewellyn's slim body folded itself over on the minimalist settee. 'I have no idea. How do you prove a negative? Everything points to you.' Llewellyn gazed steadily at Rafferty. 'You didn't kill them, did you?'

'Of course I bloody well didn't.' Rafferty was so outraged he even managed to put his own doubts behind him. 'I'm cut to the quick that you can even *ask*.' If even *Llewellyn* believed him capable of murder...

'I had to ask,' Llewellyn said. 'I needed to see your face when you denied it. Not that I really thought you guilty. Not even after I heard what Blythe said to you when I went to fetch a glass of water for your cough.'

He should have guessed that Nigel's great barn of a living room would act like a whispering gallery. 'So, you've known my secret almost as long as I have. Why didn't you say anything?'

'What would you suggest I said?' Llewellyn asked. 'I was in something of a quandary.'

That makes two of us, Rafferty thought.

'You might have behaved like a fool, but you *were* still my superior officer.'

'*Are* still your superior officer,' Rafferty amended. Though he wasn't prepared to guess how much longer that would apply. 'At least now I understand why you didn't complain about doing most of the work on the case.' This had puzzled him. But as Llewellyn explained, he had been working so hard to help *him*.

Rafferty managed a smile and the comment, 'I'm glad to know you believe me. Why is that? Because I'm such a trustworthy kind of a guy?'

'No,' was Llewellyn's blunt reply. 'It's because you always look so uncomfortable when you lie.'

'Another hang-up I can blame on the Catholic church. Anyway, how were you so sure I didn't kill those women?' Rafferty asked.

'I *did* study psychology at university,' Llewellyn reminded him. 'I've worked with you for some time now. I think I might have noticed if you'd suddenly developed psychotic tendencies. You don't possess a poker face, my dear cousin in-law. If you'd killed two girls in such a frenzied manner you wouldn't be able to conceal it for a moment. Besides, those murders were hate-filled. In your Nigel persona you had just met those young women. What possible reason could you have to hate them? You might be many things, but a psychopath you're not. Besides, your stern Catholic conscience wouldn't let you rest if you were guilty.'

That was true, Rafferty acknowledged.

Why hadn't it occurred to *him* that his conscience would have given him no peace till he had given himself up? Llewellyn's words were a great comfort after all the self-torture and doubt. Relieved, Rafferty slumped back in his seat. 'Anyway, now you know I'm innocent—'

'I didn't say you were *innocent*,' Llewellyn broke in. 'Far from it, from what you've just told me. I only meant you're innocent of murder at least.'

'Whatever.' Rafferty wasn't interested in swapping pedantic semantics with Llewellyn. He knew he'd lose. 'So I can take it, that being the case, that you won't shop me?'

Llewellyn raised perfectly arched eyebrows. 'Is that what you think of *me*?'

Rafferty didn't answer. What could he say? That, yes, he did believe the high-minded, high-moral-ground Llewellyn capable of shopping him to Superintendent Bradley? Now was not the time for games of truth or dare. He was just relieved Llewellyn was going to keep his secret. At least, that was what he'd *thought* Llewellyn had said. But Llewellyn's next words made clear he'd got hold of the wrong idea entirely.

'No. I won't *shop you*, as you call it. Because you're going to go to Superintendent Bradley yourself and tell him what you've told me.'

Rafferty's jaw dropped. 'Am I hell as like.

No way,' he insisted when he'd got over the shock. 'Confess all that to Bradley? I'd rather be arrested, tried and banged up.'

'It might yet come to that, of course. But you're going to have to come off the Lonely Hearts case in any event.'

'I'm buggered if I will! I'm committed to this case. And now that I've finally got some leads—'

'Leads? What leads?'

Rafferty, intent on arguing his case, waved aside Llewellyn's question. 'We both know what would happen if I do as you suggest. Bradley'll suspend me. After he's thrown the book at me, that is. Or he would, if I told him. Which I'm not going to do.'

Llewellyn's dark eyes regarded him steadily till Rafferty sighed and he asked plaintively, 'Am I?'

By a rare piece of luck, when Rafferty *did* go to see Bradley, his secretary told him the superintendent had that morning gone off to attend a management conference to learn advanced techniques in covering his own arse. Only she had used the official title: *Management and the Art of Intelligent Delegation.*

Briefly, he flirted with the idea of forgetting all about reporting his misdeeds, but as he'd primed himself up to 'tell all', he had to tell *somebody*. So Rafferty gladly by-passed

Bradley and went above his head to the Deputy Assistant Chief Constable, Jack Mulcahy.

Mulcahy had a well-earned reputation for being a bit of a bad lad in his younger days. He certainly wasn't one of the politically correct brigade, for which Rafferty was thankful. He was thankful also that Jack Mulcahy had risen so high in spite of blotting his copy-book a few times. It would, Rafferty believed as he was shown into Mulcahy's plush office, make him more understanding of the follies of others. Or so he hoped.

'You're a bloody idiot, Rafferty,' Mulcahy told him, when he'd stumbled his way to the end. 'What are you?'

'A bloody idiot, sir,' Rafferty repeated obediently.

'You're a grown man or supposed to be. Why didn't you just tell your mother to keep her nose out of your business?'

Mulcahy was a man reputed to never let anyone get the upper hand; certainly not his mother. From the iron-grey filings of his hair, to his pugnacious jaw-line, he had the kind of face that terrified ne'er-do-wells and made the police PR team despair.

Rafferty hated to think he was being marked down in Mulcahy's eyes. He protested as vehemently as he dared. 'I *do* tell her, sir. She just doesn't take any notice.'

'Get yourself another wife, Rafferty, one capable of keeping your mother in line. Or put in for a transfer to another part of the country.'

'Getting another wife was why I joined the dating agency in the first place, sir,' Rafferty quietly reminded him. 'Look where that's landed me. And as for moving away, knowing Ma, she'd up sticks and follow me.'

Mulcahy raised bristling eyebrows. 'Stalker, is she, your mother?'

Rafferty smiled. 'No, not really. It just feels like it sometimes.'

Mulcahy stared pityingly at him before he said briskly, 'Right, here's what we're going to do about all this.'

Sixteen

Rafferty pulled the door of Mulcahy's office to behind him with a gentle click. He wanted to whoop out loud, but restrained himself. Mulcahy had decided to do very little. Keen to hush up Rafferty's folly, he had even opted to keep him in charge of the Lonely Hearts investigation.

'It gives you an advantage,' the pragmatic Mulcahy had told him. 'It's seldom we get one of those. Use it.' He had even come down firmly against telling Bradley about their conversation.

Rafferty could scarcely believe his luck. He raised his eyes ceiling-ward and said a heartfelt, 'Thank you, God.'

Things at last seemed to be going his way. Because when Rafferty returned to his office and tried Lancelot Bliss again, the doctor answered on the first ring. And after Rafferty had explained what he wanted to know, Bliss proved as generous as ever with information.

'Got a flat in the town centre. Why do you ask?'

'Let's just say your comment set me thinking. Well, that and a little bird.'

'What little bird's that, Inspector? Not a nice little uniformed one? I'm partial to a uniform myself. If she's got a friend—'

'Not that kind of bird,' Rafferty told him before he said goodbye and put the phone down.

He finally believed he was getting to the crux of the case. After all the lies, complications and evasions he was convinced he was almost there and that the difficulties were behind him. He had the dots. It was just a matter of joining the last of them to the rest. For the first time since the case had begun, he was feeling confident, in control, on top of things. That was why the second phone call was such a shock. It came out of the blue. The first one, of course, he'd been expecting – and dreading – for days.

Nigel had rung Kylie Smith and discovered his alibis were now useless. When Rafferty had finally managed to get him to stop ranting and raving, Nigel had admitted he hadn't been with either woman at the relevant times. He'd actually been sleeping with his boss's wife – something he'd been understandably keen to keep quiet, which was why Kylie and Kayleigh had obliged him with alibis. They had at first thought it a bit of a laugh, but that attitude hadn't outlived Smales's letting of the cat and her entire litter out of the bag. Unfortunately, Nigel confided, from an alibi point of view, his boss's wife was proving obstinate.

'Selfish bitch won't say a word to get me out from under,' Nigel had bitterly complained. 'I wouldn't mind so much, but she admitted she'd never had such a good time between the sheets. I won't be supplying her with multiple orgasms again in a hurry, I can tell you.'

It was a pity about the alibi. Rafferty suspected Nigel thought so, too, especially since it meant his prowess between the sheets wouldn't get the airing he seemed to think it deserved. But he had managed to put Nigel off from going to see the brass till the following morning. He still had hopes of appeasing him.

No, it was the second phone call that had really worried him. He had been in his office, quietly thinking through his next move on the Nigel front, when in a few words, all his plans, all his expectations, had been destroyed. He knew he had to face what he had feared all along – exposure. Having to prove he wasn't a murderer. Unfortunately, that was the one thing he couldn't prove. As Llewellyn had said – how could one prove a negative?

'Inspector. How strange *you* should answer Nigel Blythe's mobile.'

Briefly, Rafferty had been so taken aback that he could find nothing to say. His quick glance at the back of the mobile had confirmed his error. Sure enough, there was the mobile number that Nigel had stuck on it. His hoarding instinct hadn't allowed him to dispose of it. He'd kept it at home, but somehow, between all the sleepless nights, the worry, the *drinking*, he'd rushed out that morning, late as usual, and managed to snatch up the wrong mobile.

As he put the phone back to his ear he was in time to hear Caroline Cranston say, 'Though now I think about it, it makes sense. I certainly wondered at the coincidence when two young women died shortly after you joined the agency. In fact, there are several things about you that I find rather worrying. Perhaps we should meet and you can set my mind at rest? I'm sure there must be simple explanations to the things that have been puzzling me. But if not, I suppose I can always go to see your superintendent.'

Rafferty wanted to avoid that at all costs because even though he had been to see Mulcahy, confessed all, and been told to forget it, Mulcahy had also bluntly told him that if his involvement was revealed from another source there was no way he could expect similar protection. That – and Nigel's threat – had proved sufficient spur for him to agree to meet Caroline. Not to mention the hope he still nurtured that he might yet salvage *something* from the mess.

Maybe, now she had learned his secret, Caroline would be persuaded to reveal a few of her own. He hoped – well, he wasn't sure exactly *what* he was hoping for, but he tooled himself up with a mike and recorder just the same. Rafferty didn't know how he'd persuade her to talk – he had no clear proof. All he had was a series of coincidences, some odd facts and his old friend, gut instinct, but he had a strong feeling that this meeting might be his one chance to save himself, completely exonerate his cousin and trap the murderer of two beautiful young women. It was too good an opportunity to pass up.

Conscious that he was five minutes too late in so doing, he switched off Nigel's mobile. Then, slowly, he rose and went out to meet Caroline Cranston.

Rafferty drew up at the Cranstons' gates, got out and pressed the intercom to identify himself. The gates swept back with barely a sound.

Caroline came out through the front door before he had a chance to drive his vehicle through the hedge to the side car park. She waved him down and told him, 'Leave your car here, Inspector. Guy's away in London, so he can't object.'

Rafferty did as instructed and was about to

head for the still-open front door when Caroline again stopped him.

'Let's go for a walk in the grounds. I've always liked walking at night.'

Rafferty fell in beside her. The grounds were extensive. Soon, they had breasted a small rise and left the house and its welcoming lights behind.

The April night was black as Satan's soul, the moon and stars hidden behind a deep bank of rain-clouds. Caroline didn't stumble once. Sure-footedly, she led Rafferty to a small glade behind the trees and stopped.

Dead autumn leaves were still on the ground. Rafferty kicked at a pile and uncovered a dead animal. It was small and too far gone in decay to tell what kind of creature it had once been. He shuddered, and moved away.

Suddenly, he felt the cold clammy hand of fear clutch his heart. Was this how Estelle had felt, he wondered, when she realised all her hopes and dreams were about to end? Jenny, too, had met death all unready for it.

Rafferty told himself he was being foolish; the clutch of the clammy hand was probably no more than a throwback to his childhood when he'd had a fear of the dark. He'd forgotten how densely black a moonless country night could be; easy to understand why he and countless superstitious generations before him shared such an atavistic emotion. God knew he had plenty of things to fear tonight; like the loss of his career and his freedom. He didn't think losing his life was likely to be numbered amongst them.

That was why it came as such a shock when he saw the gun appear in Caroline's hand. Noticed how steadily she held it. Now he understood why some primitive bodily instinct had warned him he had reason to be afraid. It wasn't much consolation to know he had been right in his conviction that Caroline Cranston was the double murderer.

'So, Inspector – or should I call you Mr Blythe?'

Her words brought back clearly to Rafferty his early conviction that Caroline Cranston was the one most likely to see through his disguise. But in true Libran style he'd chosen to bury the anxiety. Now, too late, he realised she had known from the start that he wasn't Nigel Blythe. Unfortunately, he thought he understood her motives for keeping his secret. He wished he didn't. It was a suspicion she confirmed when he asked her if she *had* known.

'I have a very good eye for faces,' she told him. 'It was clear to me when I looked at the photograph on your document that you weren't the real Nigel Blythe. Whoever he is, he has a certain style that you lack.'

Mockingly, she added, 'I imagine his suits fit him rather better, too.'

'So why—?'

'Why didn't I say so at once and put an end to your foolish charade? Surely you've worked that out by now?'

Rafferty suspected he had, but he let her explain anyway.

'You suited my requirements perfectly. I knew immediately I would be able to make use of you. I'd been planning it all for some time, you see. And when I discovered you were a policeman it fitted my plans even better. It gave you so much more to lose. You really have told an awful lot of lies, haven't you, Inspector? Do you think anyone will believe you didn't commit suicide when you knew you were about to be exposed as a double murderer?'

'But we both know I didn't kill those girls,' Rafferty protested automatically, too shocked by her revelation of his fate to be able to find a stronger argument. 'No one will believe—'

'They'll believe all right,' she cut in sharply. 'Do you really think me so foolish not to have made sure of it? But this isn't about you, though before you start protesting your virtue, perhaps you ought to reflect on the thought that, but for your own deception, you wouldn't be in this situation. No. This is about the faithless husband that

I used to love so deeply.'

'A case of love to hatred turn'd?'

'Precisely. And when, after your death, it's revealed – as it will be, I made sure of that as well – that Guy had been seeing both of those dead trollops I will retract my statement that gives him an alibi. Once your colleagues check him out, they'll find it's *his* DNA on their skin and clothes – fibres from his clothes and the hair from his head – my faithless husband will go to jail for a very long time.'

Caroline smiled. It was a smile to chill the soul and make one believe that – if there wasn't a God – there was certainly a Devil abroad on the Earth.

'Not that he'll be able to stand it in jail. Guy is used to the finer things in life. I know him, you see, so well. He'll commit suicide before a year is out and then I'll be a very rich widow. When I killed his first wife I thought I'd be able to get Guy to marry me. I was right about that. But as I discovered, all I got was the man, not his love or the faithful behaviour his first wife enjoyed. Still, I haven't come out of it too badly. I'll be free to sell *her* house, the house Guy loved and which I've always hated. Free to burn all my predecessor's ghastly tat and those amateur daubs Guy fondly calls *art*. Free, according to my Catholic faith, to marry again and have the children Guy always denied me.'

It was a warped, twisted, but very Catholic logic. The kind of logic that prompted the slaughter during the Spanish Inquisition and the burnings at Smithfield during Mary Tudor's reign; executions which had been carried out with such pious rectitude that, when he had read the accounts, Rafferty had wondered at the unchristian hypocrisy of it all and that intelligent beings had managed to convince themselves such slaughter was God's work.

The same kind of logic, which wouldn't permit Caroline to divorce her philandering husband, had no difficulty in approving an Old Testament exacting of vengeance in killing two young women, framing one foolish man and murdering another.

It was the kind of logic, too, that would kill Jenny Warburton without mercy, but that wouldn't permit the dishonesty of putting her credit card through the machine and 'charging' her for her non-existent membership of the agency.

It explained, too, why Estelle's body hadn't been nearly as brutalised as Jenny's. Jenny had dared to trespass on Caroline's home *and* husband, even if home and husband were both hated and Jenny hadn't known that Guy was married 'till Isobel had mentioned it. In all innocence, she had come to spend a loving evening with her boyfriend. No wonder she had gone quiet when

Rafferty turned up, swiftly followed by a hundred more lonely hearts and her boy-friend's wife. No wonder either that she had been so short with Guy immediately after. Truly, she had gone like a lamb to the slaughter.

Rafferty wondered whether Caroline would feel any remorse if he told her that Jenny had been an innocent. Somehow, he doubted it. Caroline was too far gone down the hatred and revenge road to allow herself any compassion or regret for the death of one innocent girl and one – Estelle – perhaps not so innocent.

The last pieces of the puzzle now clicked into place and he understood why Estelle, too, had been murdered. Isobel had been right when she had said she thought Estelle had been trying to prove something in dating so many men on the agency's books. Now it was clear to Rafferty that she had signed up with the agency, dated the men, so she could do so right under Guy's nose. She had wanted to prove that other men found her attractive and to make Guy jealous after he had dumped her. She had succeeded on both counts. But it hadn't been only Guy's jealousy she had stimulated. That brief triumph had ensured her death.

Isobel had had a lucky escape. Because Rafferty didn't doubt she would have been the third victim of Caroline's jealous rage and determination to punish Guy. No wonder she had fled to her parents' home, feeling as if 'someone has walked over my grave'. Better for her if she had stayed there because Rafferty believed Caroline might just be mad enough to kill again if her plans for himself and Guy went smoothly.

Lance Bliss's comment that Isobel had made nuisance phone calls to Guy had prompted him to ask Bliss which number she had rung, unable to believe that even Isobel would be so blatant as to ring Guy and Caroline's home, especially when Guy was hardly ever there and it was likely to be Caroline who answered. Nor could he see the urbane and sophisticated Guy Cranston being foolish enough to hand out his mobile number to his occasional bed companions. It was then that Lance had told him about the *pied-à-terre* Guy kept in town. That realisation had helped, of course, but it was the memory of his ma's baited slug traps that had given him most of the rest.

Caroline had deliberately set up the venue 'error' in order to catch Guy out. Like Ma with her beer slug-catcher, she had baited her trap, giving Guy to think she would be out for the entire evening and the house was his to do what he would. No wonder when he had walked in on them Guy had looked at him oddly as if wondering what Rafferty was doing there. At the time, Rafferty had felt so self-conscious and anxious that he had assumed Guy had seen through his borrowed designer suit to the unsophisticated copper that lay beneath and had considered showing him the door.

The way Guy had smoothed over this initial awkwardness and made him welcome had put the scene from his mind. But when put together with the rest everything became clear.

Guy had fallen neatly, predictably, into each one of the traps Caroline had set for him. She had even, when questioned by Llewellyn, provided Guy with an alibi for both murders. She had told Llewellyn that Guy had been with her for fifteen minutes either side of the suspected murder times. She had arranged these alibis deliberately to fool her husband into thinking she was desperate to protect him from police suspicions. He had probably even been grateful. Because they would both know the police would have him down as a serious suspect if they discovered he had been the lover of both murdered girls.

In reality, of course, Caroline had used her husband to provide herself with an alibi until such time as it suited her to expose him.

Caroline had already killed three people. Rafferty was wondering why she was taking so long to claim her fourth when he saw her steady her grip with her other hand. Now, he told himself, it's *your* turn to die.

The shot, when it finally came, was a head shot. He felt a searing pain at his temple and began to fall. But before eternity darkened his vision he had the satisfaction of knowing the microphone had recorded every damning word of her admission.

Seventeen

Fortunately, his 'thick Irish skull', as Sam Dally liked to describe it, had saved him from serious injury. Well, that and Llewellyn.

Later, when Caroline had been handcuffed and placed in the back of the police car summoned by Llewellyn, his sergeant explained, while they awaited the ambulance, that he had seen Rafferty leave in his car from the police car park and had followed him to 'have a little talk' with him. It had been his flying tackle that had ruined Caroline's aim.

Although Caroline had stayed silent ever since being restrained and bundled into the police car, Rafferty thought it unlikely her silence would long endure. She would want to strike out, to hurt and damage as many people as she could. Her lonely life within an unfaithful marriage had helped to turn her obsessive nature into that of a killer. But no, that couldn't be right, he told himself through waves of dizziness. Hadn't she admitted killing Guy's first wife?

Perhaps her nature had its roots deep in childhood. The unloved, criticised child that

Rafferty suspected she had been had turned into an unloved woman, unable, by her very nature, to keep the love of her 'on-the-rebound' husband.

But maybe he'd be lucky. As the pragmatic Jack Mulcahy had remarked after Llewellyn had got him on the phone to tell him what had happened, 'I wouldn't worry. I reckon you'll get away with it. The woman is clearly barking, so who'd believe her? I doubt she'll be considered fit to ever stand trial. Count your blessings, Rafferty, and learn from them.'

After having kept his own shameful secret for so long, it was a relief to Rafferty to know he could confide in Llewellyn. He was surprised when the Welshman didn't tell him how wrong-headed he had been.

All Llewellyn said was, 'You didn't need to feel so alone, you know. You're always welcome at our home. I thought you knew that.'

'And you just back from honeymoon?'

'Honeymoons don't last for ever,' Llewellyn told him portentously. 'As a matter of fact, we thought we might start entertaining. Do you feel you might be up to a dinner party next week? Only I have a cousin I'd rather like you to meet.'

'This cousin – Welsh is she?'

'Not quite, no.'

Rafferty frowned at this, but let it pass. 'And what's this cousin called?'

‘Abra. I *did* offer to introduce you to her before if you remember,’ Llewellyn reminded him. ‘But from what you’ve said in the past you abhor any attempts at matchmaking.’

Rafferty nodded. He remembered now. It had been this Abra that Llewellyn had been trying to fix him up with on the morning of his wedding and on several occasions since. ‘Blame Ma. She’s the reason I don’t like anyone trying to matchmake for me. I mean, look at Ma’s efforts. Did you know she thought at one time that me and your Maureen would make a natural couple?’

‘No,’ said Llewellyn. He blinked and stared at Rafferty as if he was having trouble absorbing the idea. ‘What decided her against the idea?’

‘*I* did,’ Rafferty told him. ‘And aren’t you glad I did? Maureen’s far more your sort of girl. But if Ma had got her way, it might have been Maureen and *me* just back from honeymoon.’

It was ironic really, Rafferty thought as he fought against the increasing dizziness. After all the traumas he’d endured since joining the dating agency to avoid his ma’s matchmaking endeavours, he was now the proud possessor of *two* matchmakers. Strangely, he felt an unexplained certainty that the efficient Welshman would be the better of the two.

Llewellyn gave the brief, uncertain smile of the unpractised matchmaker. 'Abra's name, at least, should please Mrs Rafferty.'

'Oh? Why's that?'

'It means "Mother of Multitudes".'

'Mother of Multitudes!' was Rafferty's last coherent thought, before he gave in to the growing waves of blackness and fainted.

Rafferty was nervous. It was the night of Llewellyn and Maureen's dinner party. At least, this time, he could attend the party as himself, in his own clothes, his own name and with his own accent. Please God, he thought, tonight I won't be involved in murder.

He readjusted his burdens of wine and flowers and was reaching out his finger to press the doorbell. But before he could do so the door was yanked open. He had expected Llewellyn to answer the door – he was usually punctilious in fulfilling the social duties of a host. But tonight, instead of Llewellyn, he was greeted by an elfin, dark-haired girl in bare feet.

'Oh. You must be "The Inspector", as Dawdlin' calls you. For some reason he always seems to say it in capitals. I'm Abra.' She eyed the bandage wrapped round his head. 'He said you'd been in the wars, though he wouldn't tell me why.'

Rafferty was relieved to hear it. He felt

enough of a fool already without the world, his wife and Llewellyn's *cousin* knowing just how much of an idiot he'd been. But he supposed, in a way, he should be grateful to Caroline Cranston. If she hadn't shot him, the doctors might never have found the blood clot on his brain that had been causing the blackouts and forgetfulness. 'Dawdlin''?' he queried as the name penetrated the bandages.

'What I call my cousin, Davy. Don't get me wrong. Guy's a sweetheart. But his innate caution makes him slower than a hibernating tortoise. He's never learned how to let his life jive.' She opened the cigarette pack she held, saw it was empty and swore. 'I left home in a rush. I thought I had *two* full packs.'

Rafferty plunged his hand into his off-licence carrier bag and pulled out the smoker's equivalent of the nursery rhyme plum. 'Have these.' Strangely, that very afternoon, he had broken his cigarette ban and bought sixty strong ones. After his Made In Heaven experiences, taking up smoking again seemed a safer use of his cash than using the money saved to sign up with another dating agency.

Abra's dark eyes lit up when she saw the cigarettes. 'You darling man. I think I love you already. Dawdlin' said I would.'

'Did he?'

'Mm,' she murmured as she removed the cellophane from the cigarette packet. 'Told me we were probably a match,' she struck against the side of the Swan Vestas and drew smoke deep into her lungs, 'made in heaven.'

Briefly, Rafferty closed his eyes. When he opened them again, he saw Abra was looking intently at his rattling carrier bag.

'Thank God. You've brought more booze,' she said. 'Not only a plentiful supply of fags but decent-sized bottles, too. I could kiss you.'

'I don't think your cousin would approve on such a short acquaintance.'

'Dafyd can be such a stuff-pot,' she agreed before she turned on her heel. 'Hang on to that.' She handed him her burning cigarette with the instruction, 'Stay there. I'll get us some glasses.' She was back in moments. She sat down on the front step and patted the place beside her. 'Take a pew.'

'Shouldn't we go in?' Rafferty asked.

'God, no. Davy's still fussing over the wine. The red's too cold apparently and the white's too warm. Still not allowed to drink either of them.' She looked sideways at him. 'Hope you're not so fussy?'

Rafferty shook his head. 'All I require of wine is that it's wet and makes me maudlin'.'

'Me, too. Besides, you don't imagine Davy allows *smoking* indoors?'

Rafferty was only too well acquainted with

the fact.

'Why do you think I came out here?' She made as if to rise. 'Do you need a corkscrew?'

'No. I always buy screw-tops. Saves time.'

'Ditto. So much easier.' She settled back on the doorstep, her shoulder pressed companionably against his. 'You sound like a man after my own heart.'

And as he loosened the screw-top, Rafferty believed that Llewellyn might just be right. Again. After his recent tragic brush with romance, Rafferty had made the firm decision to put thoughts of improving his love life on hold. But now, with his typical swift Libran shift from one viewpoint to its opposite, he realised his decision had been weak. Didn't they say you should get back on a horse immediately after a fall?

Not that Abra bore any resemblance to a horse; not, he amended, if you discounted her hair, which she wore in a long, shining plait that reached halfway down her back, or her legs, which were long and slender.

He poured the wine and lit her second cigarette. 'Dafyd tells me your name means "Mother of Multitudes",' he told her. 'Will you be, do you think?'

'Not bloody likely.'

Rafferty smiled and leaned back against her shoulder. For, after all, as he told himself happily, his ma didn't need to know that.